Fleur
of Yesterday

Also by Susan Marshall

Fiction

The Makeshift Girl series:
Makeshift Girl: The Secret Heritage Trail

Poetry

Evergold Dream

Plays

Indigo's Haven

Broken World

Fleur
of Yesterday

SUSAN MARSHALL

Published in Australia in 2023 by
Story Playscapes
Victoria, Australia
ABN 62197863313

publications@storyplayscapes.com
www.storyplayscapes.com

 A catalogue record for this book is available from the National Library of Australia

Title: Fleur of Yesterday
Series: Theatre Playscapes Series: No.1
Author: Susan Marshall
ISBN: 9780645404142
Subjects: Young Adult Fiction / Performing Arts / General
          Young Adult Fiction / Performing Arts / Theatre & Musicals
          Young Adult Fiction / Science Fiction / Time Travel

Produced by Story Playscapes

Written by Susan Marshall

Book design, photography and digital art by Ryan Marshall

All images Copyright © Story Playscapes

For my loving husband, Ryan and my beautiful daughter, Arlia.
I will always love and cherish our moments together.

Contents

In her article: *Theatre Playscapes: A New Theatrical Style*, award-winning Susan Marshall draws upon her extensive experiences as a professional author, theatre practitioner and expert educator to discuss the development of her new theatrical style: Theatre Playscapes and how she used it to create *Fleur of Yesterday*.

Theatre Playscapes
A New Theatrical Style

The twenty first century marks an unprecedented emphasis on individualism within the constraints of globalisation. The profound result has been a dramatic shift in the ways we grow and gain senses of identity in the world. In our brave new world, the role of the theatre is vital in its abilities to empower us to choose to nurture our beings. As a non-realistic theatrical style, Theatre Playscapes can attune us to the energetic motions of our own special moments. By interacting with such moments, we can create theatre that explores the spirits of our characters in their lifeworlds.

As a young child, my favourite type of play was to attune myself to moments of energetic motions in my lifeworlds. It was independent play and my way of learning to find my way in the world autonomously. I was drawn to evocative moments, such as a bird spanning its wings before flight or the journey of a kite flying in the air. The motions of the wind or sea could always calm me and draw my attention to aspects of my natural environment, like leaves gently dropping from tree branches or the crests of waves in the ocean. I had an ability to connect physically with such moments, which made them my comfortable and chosen playscapes.

As an adult, I notice the overstimulated cycles and routines associated with globalisation. They can leave many of us feeling disconnected from our senses of self and identity. My playful nature has remained with me my whole life. Even now, I still attune myself to moments of energetic motions, which allow me to engage with life independently. My playscapes have been essential to help me to find moments of peace and creativity. I use inspirations gained from my interactions with such playscapes, to create theatrical performance work, especially through playwriting.

It cannot be underestimated how important the act of 'play' is in our lives. There are many theories centred around the significance of child play particularly. The neurologist and founder of psychoanalysis, Sigmund Freud in his book, *Beyond the Pleasure Principle*, stated that:

> "It can be seen that in play children repeat everything that has made a great impression on them in life, and that here they are abstracting the strength of that impression – mastering the situation, as it were."[1]

Freud's emphasis on life impressions is significant. Children, with their abilities to focus with more intensity on moments of play, allow themselves to form and express such impressions of their lifeworlds. It is this focus that seems to dissipate as we grow older and become immersed in the more demanding, external streams of life.

The psychologist, Jean Piaget, in his theory of cognitive development, helps us to better understand how children form intelligence. In his book, *The Psychology of Intelligence,* he stated:

> "We shall simply say then that every action involves an energetic or affective aspect and a structural or cognitive aspect, which, in fact, unites the different points of view already mentioned."[2]

Piaget's quote emphasises how essential our very presence is in our worlds: our instinctive, cognitive and energetic responses to stimuli, help us to form our understandings of our worlds and ways to interact with them. Our responses are unique to our own ways of being and should be nurtured to enable us to continue to grow.

During my extensive experiences with young people in theatrical, community and educational settings, I have witnessed that their desires to engage in play remains vital to their personal growth, as well as the development of their personal motivations, well into young adulthood. The psychologist, Abraham Maslow, in his book: *Towards a Psychology of Being,* reflects on the importance of growth motivation in further developing the individual:

> "In such people gratification breeds increased rather than decreased motivation, heightened rather than lessened excitement. The appetites become intensified and heightened. They grow upon themselves and instead of wanting less and less, such a person wants more and more of, for instance, education. The person rather than coming to rest becomes more active. The appetite for growth is whetted rather than allayed by gratification. Growth is, in itself, a rewarding an exciting process, e.g. the fulfilling yearnings and ambitions [...]"[3]

Theatre and the sense of community it nurtures, is a special place for a young person. Along with its many benefits, it can help to guide a young adult's growing awareness of and interaction with the larger world in ways that motivate them to develop confidently within it.

A glance at our world in the twenty first century, will help us to recognise the pressing importance of us continuing to encourage growth motivation in our young people. We may begin with a focus on the impacts of individualism in our societies. The philosopher, Alexis de Tocqueville (1805-1859) in his book, *Democracy in America,* once recognised that individualism involved: "each citizen to isolate himself from his fellows and to draw apart with his family and friends,"[4] Furthermore, Tocqueville recognised that such behaviour diminished "the virtues of public life."[5] Tocqueville's description has been exaggerated in our current societies, where one may now retreat individually and seek to discover or express oneself within a mass, global context.

Globalisation itself and its influences on the rapid capital and technological growth of the world, has resulted in a major emphasis placed on individualism within globalisation's constraints. As Anthony Elliott and Charles Lemert discuss in their book: *The New Individualism: The Emotional Costs of Gobalisation:*

> "What is unmistakable about the rise of individualist culture, in which constant risk-taking and an obsessive preoccupation with flexibility rules, is that individuals must continually strive to be more efficient, faster, leaner, inventive and self-actualizing than they were previously - not sporadically, but day-in day-out."[6]

Globalisation and its emphasis on individualism poses a paradox for young adults. As they become more aware of the bigger world at large, they are keen to remain at play and to understand it. However, within the constraints of globalisation, they must increasingly do so individually. The heightened, technological focus of our societies, has led to a positive reinforcement of the isolated self in communication, whether that be through social media, the Internet or other technological or media forms.

The Australian Bureau of Statistics in their current report: *Retail Trade, Australia: April 2023*, details the retail expenditure per month, for different industry groups. If we look at the increase of such expenditure on individualised items from 1982 to 2023, we can see that the trend to purchase personal items, such as clothing, footwear and personal accessories has increased:

April, 1982: $359.9 million
April, 2023: $2837.2 million

Comparatively, the report also details the expenditure per month of household goods, which includes electronic goods. We can see how such purchasing has increased over time:

April, 1982: $592.3 million
April, 2023: $5130.7 million

Online retailing has also increased for consumers over time, with the report detailing the growth over the last four years:

April 2019: $1513.8 million
April 2023: $3357.8 million[7]

What these figures reveal is that the cultural emphasis on individualism has led to higher retail sales of items of personal value. In our brave new world, a person may desire clothing, cosmetics, electronic appliances and mobile phones, etc. These items set the trend of the individual being better, faster, more mobile, efficient and in trend, in order to make their own personal mark within the constraints of globalisation. There is also no need to visit local shops anymore, as one can simply purchase their individually desired items online.

Our young people have become inundated with the resulting sense of detachment from the world, that such a heightened preoccupation with individualism results in. As Anthony Elliott and Charles Lemert discuss further:

> "Perhaps the most distinctive feature of the new individualism is the playing out of these positive and negative features - the cultural trends towards freedom and alienation - against a backcloth of the demise of social context. Today, the people in the polished cities of the West make sense of experience on the edge of a *disappearance of context*. As science and new technologies offer alternative paradigms and possibilities for social life, we have replaced the old contexts of tradition and custom with a focus on our individual selves. This shift of focus from the old rules and boundaries to the internal world of the individual is now central to the contemporary mood. The main legacy of this cultural trend is that individuals are increasingly expected to produce context for themselves."[8]

The disappearance of familiar contexts is concerning for our young people. Senses of belonging and connection to traditions and communal approaches to life are essential to a young person's holistic development.

In our world, there is also a confusion of guidance for young people, which can be discovered electronically. The focus on individuality is now a do-it-yourself approach, which is heightened to celebrity status. The media even goes as far to suggest that one should change whatever they do not like about themselves, via cosmetic surgery or other means. The Internet and social media also provide access to inappropriate and potentially harmful content for young people. Obsession with social media and personal technologies, also work to encourage instant gratification and to limit face-to-face communication. This in turn works to further exacerbate senses of isolation and detachment from the world at large.

The Australian Psychological Society issued a media release on 27 November, 2022, titled: *Children 18 months to 18 years showing serious mental health issues, APS survey reveals*. I quote their findings below:

> "The October survey of more than one thousand Australian psychologists asked them to list presenting issues in their patients compared with two years prior. Children were grouped into three categories, 18 months to 5 years, 6-12 years, and 13-18 years.

> "All three age groups showed significant increases in mental illness and disorders across a range of symptoms.

> "We are sleepwalking into a social and economic disaster unless we act decisively" Dr Davis-McCabe said.

> "We risk a lost generation of young people who will never be able to realise their dreams should their mental ill-health continue to spiral undertreated or untreated at all.

"You don't get a second chance to relive your childhood and develop into a mentally healthy and capable adult.

"A coordinated and sustained effort of prevention and early intervention to avert the worst of this crisis is desperately needed before it's too late."[9]

The Australian Psychological Society's call to action is necessary in a time where our young people are needing more support than ever. In this age of heightened individualism, we must realise our communal roles as members of larger societies, to help our young people to feel safe and cared for.

Theatre is vital in the way that its community can empower our young people to play, engage and grow within the familiar contexts of their lives. However, to continue to support young people in the twenty first century, the theatre must take into account the dichotomy between a young person's natural, increasing independence and the pervading pressures of individualism saturating young people's day to day lives.

If we return to our earlier discussion, we can reflect on Piaget's emphasis on the importance of both cognitive and energetic aspects of actions. In my range of extensive theatrical experiences with young adults, I have witnessed their needs to understand and justify their ideas before energetically engaging with them.

As a non-realistic theatrical style, Theatre Playscapes allows for both cognitive and energetic explorations and responses to the worlds in which we live. One way to attune a young person's desires towards nurturing oneself and to eventually feel safe in autonomy, is to remove the pressures of individualism within the constraints of globalisation.

Theatre Playscapes empowers a young person to begin to connect with the reliable, conservational energies of their lifeworld. To begin to use the theatrical style, I suggest stepping outside at first and witnessing the natural motions of energies at play. An example may be the gentle, kinetic fluttering of butterfly wings or the soothing, radiant energy of the sun on the skin. There are many natural energies in motion that one can witness and/or experience an interaction with. In this way, a young person is able to take gentle, self directed steps towards gaining a healthy, independent connection with the natural world. One's own natural and instinctive connections to such energies will also begin to nurture one's wonderful spirit. Rich stories and performance work can also be conceived through such nurturing times.

Energy pulses all around us. As Robert L Jaffe and Washington Taylor state in their book: *The Physics of Energy*:

"Energy is ubiquitous. We see it in the motion of the world around us – the flow of the water, wind and waves, the violence of volcanic eruptions and the intense activity of small animals – and we feel it in the warmth of the air and water in our environment."[10]

The conservational nature of energy made it a reliable thing for me to engage with as a child. For example, I could rely on the fact that wind had particular energetic motions and that gave me senses of comfort and peace as I explored the moments of my lifeworlds. Energy is something that can be researched easily and justified cognitively by a young person. Energy can also be explored through practical performance, creatively and energetically.

I have explored many forms of energy in my theatrical works, leading to my development of the non-realistic, theatrical convention: **heightened energy.** Special moments for characters in performance are heightened in their kinetic, potential, radiant, thermal, sonic, electrical or gravitational energy. Note that I mention 'moments,' to help give focus to one's instinctive or independent connection to an energy form for a special period of time. Moments are so precious in our fast paced and over saturated society. They allow us to attune more powerfully with our beings and senses of self.

When I was in France, energy's motion, formed my first initial concepts for *Fleur of Yesterday*. Visiting the beautiful Luberon village of Lourmarin, I climbed a stunning series of rock steps up to a small hill. The kinetic energy of the wind was mesmerising, attuning me to its ribbon-like motions through the air. Immersing myself silently in the hill's playscape, I lifted my arms up into the air in order to absorb the wind's rhythms. It was a spiritual and uplifting moment in my own life, yet one that was also instrumental in the germination of my beginning ideas for the play.

I acknowledge an inspirational quote by the philosopher, poet and environmental scientist, Henry David Thoreau, who once stated:

> "We need the tonic of wildness ... At the same time that we are earnest
> to explore and learn all things, we require that all things be mysterious
> and unexplorable, that land and sea be indefinitely wild, unsurveyed
> and unfathomed by us because unfathomable. We can never have enough
> of nature."[11]

In my independence, I have also nurtured a passion for Romanticism, which is also inspirational for my writing. As a modern Romanticist, I believe that the untamed wildness in both natural and human spirits should be nurtured and celebrated.

Returning to my moment of physical connection with the wind, I experienced its velocity propelling towards me at a rapid speed. It struck me with great force, winding me and pushing my body forward. After a moment, I stood once more and discovered that I was facing grassland by the hillside. I watched as the wind's strong motion pulled stems of grass and wild flower heads temporarily backwards with its own force. I considered how dependent on the wind, the wild flowers and I had been in our own respective moments.

Luckily, the wild flowers still remained standing, their roots firmly planted within the soil.

Stepping forward, I immersed myself in the grassland, engaging with the variety of wild flowers that I saw. Their wind blown, kinetic energies enticed me to study and appreciate their gorgeous, natural states. Untouched by interventional science or commercialism, they were able to shoot meristem and *be* across the grassland. There, in my physical connection with that wild and untamed playscape, emerged my first concepts for a play that spoke for the importance of the precious life of the wild flower.

Fleur of Yesterday unravels the major, universal issue of plant breeding and its impacts on natural and human worlds. The following quote by the renown garden designer and writer, Noel Kingsbury in his book, *Hybrid: The History & Science of Plant Breeding,* emphasises the significance of this issue globally:

> "Improving upon nature is the very essence of plant breeding, so it goes to the heart of one of the central debates of the human condition: the relationship between humanity and nature and the degree to which the human race has the right (or indeed the responsibility) to change plant life for its own ends."[12]

The journeys of Fleur and her Carnation flower provoke us to question the rights of human nature to make choices concerning the life of plants. At the heart of the play, I evoke precious moments that pulse with the fragile and vital dependencies of nature on humanity. We witness the journey of the Carnation, who, along with its friends, once existed as a wild flower on the hill of Bry. The Carnation becomes aware of a human, commercial desire for its wild form to be subjected to the sciences of intraspecific breeding and hybridisation. We may ask the questions: What impact will the acts of plant breeding have on the future of wild carnations across the meadow of Bry? Is it possible to save the wild carnation?

In the play, moments of heightened, radiant energy exist for characters, in order to emphasise their significant energetic connections with moments in their human and natural lifeworlds. Fleur is a nature whisperer and this skill returns to her instinctively at a significant moment when she attunes with the radiant energy present:

FLEUR

Closing my eyes, I listen to the silence.
It is a moment to connect with nature.
I bathe once more in the calm blue skies: 2, 3, 4,
soaking in the light rays: 4, 5, 6.

Warmth radiates from my skin.
I breathe in: 2, 3, 4 ...
Expelling my energy: 4, 5, 6,
feeding the substrate of the hill and its meadow.

The life oppressed hill creaks,
beginning to tremor beneath my feet.
I breathe in: 2, 3, 4,
trying to maintain the warmth.

Its substrate begins to burst with buds,
small, green buds that, given warmth,
accelerate rapidly in growth,
until my warmth is not needed anymore.

Standing back, I accept the echoes
of gratitude from the awakened hill.
Looking down, I await the guidance
it has rewarded me with.

Lush and green, it is life
that Maman and I know existed here once before.[13]

In the above excerpt, Fleur demonstrates that she is using a balance of cognitive and energetic responses to her lifeworld. She is at peace with her actions in this moment.

Thermal energy is also used as inspiration for this play, to create moments that generate or reflect on the effects of heat (fire) and cool (water). At the play's opening, we become aware that Fleur awakens on a bridge, surrounded by the smoky haze of a distant fire, yet does not remember how or why she came to be there. Moments of heightened thermal energy help to provide Fleur and Celia's connections with memories of heat, a key link to a major event and its proceeding aftermath.

As *Fleur of Yesterday* is a non-realistic play, my focus on characterisation is one defined by the non-realistic convention: **spirit of character** and his/her/its journeys through time. This is achieved by harnessing the energies, atmospheres, movements and rhythms of simple moments that the Carnation and other characters engage with. By doing so, I am able to demonstrate a gradual growth of their human or natural spirits as the play continues to develop. An example lies in the excerpt below:

CARNATION

Growth and senescence exists within me.
Each dawn, I am rejuvenated with the sun's glow
and with a fresh, new clove scent.
A scent that helps keep us both alert.

I feel safe upon Fleur's wrist
as she steps forward now,
her feet sinking into the fading grassland.
It has been cleared recently, I see.
Why?

My heart sinks when I think of the work
that both Fleur and Sherwin undertook
to give this grassland life, to nurture it.
Wild and free, we flowers were,
able to shoot meristem upon the hill grassland.[14]

In the above excerpt, the Carnation flower demonstrates its natural spirit through its acts of rejuvenation at dawn and its previous "wild and free" lifeworld upon the hill grassland. To further enhance the Carnation's lifeworld, I would use the non-realistic convention: **animated lifeworld**, to reveal the visual lifeworlds of the hill and grassland through performance. This can be achieved in many ways, including physical performance work, such as: mime, acrobatics, etc. It can also be achieved by the use of stagecraft: puppetry, visual projection, sound, etc. The animation of a lifeworld can lead to a performer's (and therefore character's) stronger cognitive understanding of and energetic connection with it. Such connection can also aid in developing the character's spirit.

In Lourmarin, I also had the privilege of attending the large, open-air market, which is run by the village community and is famous for its trade of exquisitely beautiful, handmade textiles, objects and food. Each trade item stored its own potential energy as a result of its position in relation to other objects or the Earth.[15] At one time, I observed a young woman viewing a white dress hanging precariously off the side of a stall. As the dress fell to the ground, releasing its potential energy, the young woman was drawn to its mesmerising beauty. Catching it mid air, she held it close to her heart and sighed.

The physical interaction of the young woman within her market playscape, led to her personal connection with the white dress. From a theatrical perspective, I could imagine her as an actor, becoming attuned to the energy and aesthetics of the costume item: a white dress. In such a moment of connection, we cannot underestimate how much the actor is able to engage with the energy released and to evoke one's own individual response.

I refer now to some text from *Fleur of Yesterday*, which reveals an evocative moment with a white dress for Celia:

CELIA
I keep returning to this moment,
it radiates like a beacon of light.
I know I am meant to discover
something important here.
No matter how much I trawl
through these remnants,
these marks of special presence,
I can't work out what it is.

AGAPANTHUS
Look straight ahead, Celia.
Can you see it, before your very eyes?
It is as white as we are,
hanging precariously over the edge of the table.

CELIA
I will try.

Yes, I see it.
It is falling to the ground.
Scarred with burn holes and marks,
yet still it floats.
It whispers gently in the wind like Fleur with all her hope.

There it lies, in a heap, on the ground.

I feel water running down my cheeks
and know that I am crying.
I am relieved to find this dress,
yet so sad at what it being here means.[16]

The non-realistic convention: **immersive language**, is used to immerse characters in their lifeworlds and moments, as well as to enhance the connection between characters. Immersive language also leaves room to allow for both cognitive and energetic responses for characters to the world through words expressed. In the previous excerpt, Celia uses such immersive language in order to reveal her spirit of character in response to the moment she discovers the white dress. The potential energy of the dress and its release, evokes memories and emotions for Celia of an important moment in the past.

Referring to the past, Fleur can revisit moments of yesterday, in an attempt to save the Carnation flower and to find her missing love, Sherwin. As she does so, she begins to become aware of the limitations and dangers of such time travel. The philosopher, Jean-Jacques Rousseau, illustrated the significant impacts of changing time on human connection/attachment in his quote from his unfinished manuscript: *Les Rêveries du Promeneur Solitaire (or The Reveries of a Solitary Walker)*:

> "Everything is in constant flux on this earth. Nothing keeps the same unchanging shape, and our affections, being attached to things outside us, necessarily change and pass away as they do. Always out ahead of us or lagging behind, they recall a past which is gone or anticipate a future which may never come into being; there is nothing solid there for the heart to attach itself to. Thus our earthly joys are almost without exception the creatures of a moment ..."[17]

The development of **transformation of moment** as a non-realistic convention, works to empower young people to work non-realistically with the constant changes that exist in life. When developing their own works, they can make decisions concerning how they could unravel such moments to tell a story through performance.

In *Fleur of Yesterday*, one way that I use transformation of moment, is to show that through transformations of yesterday's significant moments, Fleur seeks her love and connection with Sherwin. Yet, she begins to realise that yesterday can only show her so much, due to its impermanency. It is up to Fleur to find the strength to face the present.

At a larger scale, I also transform moments to show that in order for spirits of character to continue to grow, they must face challenges and adversities along their respective journeys. Therefore, transformative moments reveal how life continues to change for Fleur and other characters. In fact, moments may: blend, overlap, fleet, freeze, compliment, contrast, merge, synchronise, convert, flashback, flash-forward, etc. in order to propel dramatic action and to unravel the plot.

To assist young people with acknowledging the significance of specific situations and their impacts on life, I have also developed the non-realistic convention: **situational pull**. In such a moment, a character is being pulled towards a specific situation and may face something significant, learn new information or experience a self defining moment.

In order to develop non-realistic, transformational moments in the play, I worked to heighten their respective energies, which can also convert in form. I refer to a relevant quote from Brittanica in *Energy: Physics,* on the changing forms of energy:

"Energy can be neither created nor destroyed but only changed from one form to another."[18]

Robert L Jaffe and Washington Taylor explain this concept further:

"... each form or energy can be converted into every other form."[19]

In the above quotes, we learn that our energies in our lifeworlds are in motion and can convert to other forms. Such conversion can be used dramatically, to enhance transformational moments for characters. Here is an example in an excerpt from *Fleur of Yesterday:*

FLEUR
I am catching the drift of wind,
my body floating lightly in the sky.
Somehow, this is familiar,
as though I have sailed
through the air before.

My arms are light and free
and my body is outstretched,
kissing the blue streaks.
I can breathe freely here.
It is soothing this moment,
an elation I treasure.

I am falling, slowly now,
dropping down to the earth.
Feet landing, I exhale a breath.
I am not afraid, yet rejuvenated.

The earth is soft and luscious,
adorned with dew kissed grass.
Kicking off my shoes,
I allow my bare feet to press
into the warm earth.
Dirt catches between my toes,
comforting me with its presence.

Staring up, my eyes fall upon an apex roof
atop a glass windowed building.
It is a glasshouse, structured with a steel frame.
I sense its warm glow, inviting me to step closer.[20]

In the excerpt above, I use immersive language in order to harness moments for Fleur that transform the kinetic motions of the wind into moments exploring her own kinetic movements through the sky. These transformative moments help to reveal Fleur's connection with her lifeworld and to also reveal her spirit of character.

In the same excerpt above, using the convention: situational pull, a transformative moment involves Fleur falling from the sky and landing on the earth. The emphasis is then drawn to the situation that she is made to face, concerning the glasshouse of her past. This situation is one that unravels as a defining moment for Fleur as the play continues.

While travelling in France, I also visited the Luberon village of Rousillon, which is famous for its beautiful, ochre coloured architecture. It was a place that basked in the radiant energy of the sun and village life. I was privileged to eat food dishes created from the local produce and to become aware of the nature of village life through the wonderful people that I met. The spirits of the world and people of Rousillon stayed with me, including its gorgeous village bell. Key, simple moments of interaction with the town's energy, atmospheres and sounds also stayed with me. I used such inspirations to create fragmentary, transformative moments for the village of Bry and the setting of Fleur's significant aftermath.

Rousillon also inspired me to develop Veronique (Fleur's mother) and their special bond, which is also explored throughout transformations of moments. Veronique helps Fleur to remember her connection with her village and the significant aftermath. Veronique speaks French, her native language, which she also uses to help Fleur to remember events that have occurred. I envision that in theatrical performance, there is much opportunity to create the animated lifeworlds of Bry as a village, especially through Veronique and her connection to the aftermath.

A journey to L'Isle-sur-la-Sorgue in France, enabled me to have a chance to experience the lifeworlds of a town that flourished around and depended upon a canal. The kinetic energies of the water and its flow, along with the people engaged in the their every day lives, inspired the Romantic in me. I attuned myself to the natural spirit and kinetic energy of the water when creating a lake in Bry. It is an important location, not only for Fleur's past but also of her connection and romantic relationship with Sherwin. Her memories of life and romance with Sherwin are portrayed through the use of precious transformations of moments and heightened energy. Fleur will do all that she can to save him.

This article has demonstrated how Theatre Playscapes, as a theatrical style, has responded to the culture of globalisation and its increasing emphasis on individualism, in our world. Respecting the way that we develop through play, it recognises our needs to reach natural states of independence and later, autonomy in our lives. As such, this style also provides scope for the performer's cognitive and energetic responses to moments and situations. Overall, Theatre Playscapes provides contexts for young people to explore in ways that nurture their beings.

To summarise the Theatre Playscapes style, I am proud to provide you with an official list of its performance conventions and how to apply them. They are as follows:

HEIGHTENED ENERGY: A moment is heightened in its kinetic, potential, radiant, thermal, sonic, electrical or gravitational energy. This can be achieved through an actor's expressive skills or via the use of stagecraft. The energy's resulting velocity of motion, force or release is used to emphasise the significance of the moment for a character.

TRANSFORMATION OF MOMENT: Moments transform actively, enabling characters to develop further and to connect with their lifeworlds. Moments may: blend, overlap, fleet, compliment, contrast, freeze, convert, synchronise, flashback, flash-forward, etc. in order to enhance spiritual growth and/or propel dramatic action and/or to unravel the plot.

ANIMATED LIFEWORLD: A character's physical, emotional or psychological lifeworld is alive and animated. This works to emphasise the character's significant moments of connection and development of spirit within his/her/its lifeworld. An animated lifeworld can be achieved through a variety of techniques, such as: use of symbolic character, mime, acrobatics, aerial work, etc. It can also be achieved through stagecraft techniques, such as: puppetry, sound, lighting, visual projection, etc.

SITUATIONAL PULL: A moment where a character is pulled into a situation, e.g. falling from the sky down to earth. In this situation, his/her/its spirit of character is further developed, as they are able to face something significant and/or to learn new information and/or to experience a self-defining moment.

SPIRIT OF CHARACTER: An actor can draw upon his/her/its full range of expressive skills to demonstrate a character's natural, human, inanimate, supernatural, mechanical, fantastical or mythical spirit and its growth throughout its journey.

IMMERSIVE LANGUAGE: the language immerses characters in their lifeworlds and its moments; connections with other characters; significant emotions; moods/atmospheres, etc. Immersive language also works to provide the differing cognitive and energetic responses to moments for characters in their lifeworlds.

It has been a wonderful experience to develop the Theatre Playscapes style and to use it to create the play *Fleur of Yesterday*.

Happy discoveries!

Susan Marshall
Founder, Australian Author, Theatre Practitioner & Publisher,
Story Playscapes
4 June 2023

Performance Rights

Endnotes:

1 Freud, Sigmund (1920): *Beyond the Pleasure Principal* in Gregory C. Richter (trans. ed.) Broadview Press, 2011, p.59.

2 Piaget, Jean (1947): *The Psychology of Intelligence* in Routledge Classics (ed.), Volume 92, 1st Edition (2001).

3 Maslow, Abraham (1962) *Towards a Psychology of Being* in Start Publishing LLC (ed.), 2013.

4 Tocqueville, Alexis (1805-1859) *Democracy in America* in *Brittanica* (n.d.) 'Individualism: Politics and Philosophy.' Accessed at: https://www.britannica.com/topic/individualism

5 Tocqueville, Alexis (1805-1859) *Democracy in America* in *Brittanica* (n.d.) 'Individualism: Politics and Philosophy.' Accessed at: https://www.britannica.com/topic/individualism

6 Elliott, Anthony & Lamert, Charles (2005): *The New Individualism: The Emotional Costs of Globalization.* Routledge, p.3.

7 Australian Bureau of Statistics (April 2023): *Retail Trade, Australia: Monthly and quarterly estimates of turnover and volumes for retail businesses, including store and online sales.* Accessed at: https://www.abs.gov.au/statistics/industry/retail-and-wholesale-trade/retail-trade-australia/latest-release

8 Elliott, Anthony & Lamert, Charles (2005): *The New Individualism: The Emotional Costs of Globalization.* Routledge, p.13.

9 Australian Psychological Society (27 November, 2022) [media release]: *Children 18 months to 18 years showing serious mental health issues, APS survey reveals.* Accessed at: https://psychology.org.au/about-us/news-and-media/media-releases/2022/children-18-months-to-18-years-showing-serious-men

10 Jaffe, Robert L. & Taylor, Washington (2018): *The Physics of Energy.* Massachusetts Institute of Technology, p.3.

11 Thoreau, Henry David (1854), *Walden; Or, Life in the Woods.* Ticknor and Fields, Boston.

12 Kingsbury, Noel (2011*): Hybrid: The History & Science of Plant Breeding.* University of Chicago Press, p.7.

13 Marshall, Susan (2023): *Fleur of Yesterday.* Story Playscapes, Melbourne, Australia, p.111.

14 Marshall, Susan (2023): *Fleur of Yesterday.* Story Playscapes, Melbourne, Australia, p.52.

15 The Physics Classroom (n.d.): *Potential Energy: Work, Energy, and Power - Lesson 1 - Basic Terminology and Concepts.* Accessed at: https://www.physicsclassroom.com/class/energy/Lesson-1/Potential-Energy

16 Marshall, Susan (2023): *Fleur of Yesterday.* Story Playscapes, Melbourne, Australia, pp.69-70.

17 Rousseau, Jean-Jacques (composed between 1776-1778): *Les Rêveries du Promeneur Solitaire (or The Reveries of the Solitary Walker):* Published posthumously in *Les Confessions de J. J. Rousseau V1: Suivies Des Reveries Du Promeneur Solitaire (1782)* from Jean-Jacques Rousseau's unfinished manuscript, by Kessinger Publishing, 2009.

18 Brittanica (n.d.) *Energy: Physics.* Accessed at: https://www.britannica.com/science/energy

19 Jaffe, Robert L. & Taylor, Washington (2018): *The Physics of Energy.* Massachusetts Institute of Technology, p.4.

20 Marshall, Susan (2023): *Fleur of Yesterday.* Story Playscapes, Melbourne, Australia, p.60.

Yesterday's Wisdom

A poem written by Susan Marshall

Listen closely to the wind,
its wisdom leaps and turns,
across the years yet to unfold
and retreating into yesterday.

Wild carnation flowers emerge,
adrift in the strong gusts of wind.
Years do not trap their spirits,
which glide, soar and tumble freely.

Time does not age the shifting wind
but helps it propel old and new.
Stories are spoken high and low,
from voices beneath the breeze.

So nature and human co-exist
in this world of old and new.
Working together to discover
stories of yesterday's wisdom.

Characters

FLEUR: a time traveller, a nature whisperer.

*CARNATION: a wild flower attached to Fleur's wrist, her travel companion.

SHERWIN: Fleur's romantic partner, missing.

CELIA: a waitress, a time traveller, a friend of Fleur.

*AGAPANTHUS: flowers that accompany and assist Celia.

VERONIQUE: Fleur's mother.

PETAL: remembered as GIRL, Fleur's best friend.

*DAISIES: flowers that accompany Petal.

JARONE: a horticulturalist, a time traveller, possibly dangerous.

*ASH: accompanies Jarone. Remnant ash from yesterday.

*ELM TREE: a tree from Fleur's childhood, her protector.

*GRASS: the renewal of the land.

---

* Denotes that character may be portrayed via physical performance techniques, such as: symbolic character, acrobatics, aerial work, mime, etc. Character may also be portrayed via visual stagecraft techniques, such as: a prop, a puppet or through visual projection.

Setting

The action begins on the gold flowered bridge of the town of Bry, in a significant, present moment of the play's mystery. Proceeding transformations of moments take the audience on a journey through Fleur's reconnections with her yesterdays and lifeworlds (outside on a lawn; inside Fox Café; at the meadow and its hill; at the village lake; in the sky; at the glasshouse and during the aftermath) in order to help her spirit to grow.

The play can be staged with minimal props and set.

Act 1, Scene 1

FLEUR

A reoccurring dream …

I am potting up long stems of
wild carnation flowers.
Carefully, I pat them into the soil
with my own nurturing hands.

Gusts of fiery winds blow,
blasting a furnace of heat.
The air rings with the shrill screams
of my beloved carnations.
Rising and falling,
they shed their flower heads
upon the worn,
foot trodden dirt.

Staring up, their heads smile sadly,
their petals shedding tears.
Rolling across the planks,
they reach out for me.

The carnation flower's scent
is fragrant in the breeze.
It wakes me so I escape
the dark world of dreams.

Open up, eyes!

Smoke saturates the air.
My lungs!

I see the flames soaring high,
striking at the encroaching darkness.
Raging fire eats away at the
pink and purple hues of twilight.

Fire!

I am alone, lying on this footbridge.
The wood is rough and firm
beneath my huddled frame.

How long have I been out cold for?
What happened to me?

FLEUR

It is so hard to see through the haze.

What is that golden glint?
There are sculpted, gold wild flowers,
scattered in clustered patterns
across the metal handrails.
Staring closely, I can see daisy flowers,
carnations, lavender and agapanthus.
Flowers that grace my town, Bry's natural areas
with a beauty that I have beheld my entire life.
Each spring and summer, they draw in
crowds of onlookers from cities around the world,
who desire to gaze at their floral charm.

I can feel a churning feeling in my stomach.
Am I angry?
I wish I knew why.
My brain is in such a fog.

My throat is burning.
Tears are spilling from my eyes.
I know I need to go but …
I am drawn to …

Below, through the haze,
I can just make out
the ripples of my village lake.
It is a place I hold dear to my heart.
I feel so drawn to it.
It is a place of love for me and …

Sherwin.

Where are you?

On the bridge planks I vaguely see...
Your silver jacket lying
on the wooden path.
Its arms reach up for me.

Putting it on, I hug it tight.
I can feel you holding me.

For a moment I breathe softly,
my heart dancing in memories
of your gentle words and touch.

FLEUR
Your eyes are so blue and deep,
holding years of stories
of being on the run.
In a heartbeat, you will
always save me from trouble.

This time I must fend for myself.

Carnation, are you okay there,
wrapped around my wrist?

CARNATION
The heat has wilted me considerably, Fleur.
I don't know if I can hold on much longer.

FLEUR
How long do we have, Carnation?

CARNATION
Not too much longer, it is nearly sunset.
My scent has nearly faded.
If I am lucky, I will be revived.

FLEUR
A whole Carnation day has nearly passed.
We need to keep you alive, Carnation.

We need a fresh day.

CARNATION
Yes. A fresh day means revival for me,
along with a fresh scent.

FLEUR
We must move quickly, Carnation.
The fire is so strong!

I must pull myself up.

CARNATION
Well done, Fleur.
What can you remember?

FLEUR
I need to find a moment, don't I?

CARNATION

Yes, one we can return to safely.

FLEUR

You'll stay with me?

CARNATION

Of course.
As long as I can.

How's the thinking going?

FLEUR

I'm not used to travelling on my own.
Sherwin and I have always helped each other.
I don't know where to ...
begin.

CARNATION

Start with what you know.

FLEUR

That's easy.
Our routine.
Probably best to stick to that,
keep a low profile.

CARNATION

Sounds like a plan.

FLEUR

Breathing in Carnation's scent,
I close my eyes.
The aroma is fragrant and pure,
making my heart beat slowly.
I can see you Sherwin, in the past distance,
waiting yesterday for me.

I take one more sniff of the scent
and drift backwards into ...
A day yesterday.

Act 1, Scene 2

FLEUR

We're here, Carnation.
It is the Fox Café,
Sherwin and my favourite place.
Are you okay?

CARNATION

Clear air, such a relief.
My petals are rejuvenating once more.
It was a narrow escape.

FLEUR

Yes, thank goodness you're okay.
I don't know what I would have done if -

CARNATION

Let's not imagine the worst.
It's important for us to keep going, Fleur.
Time will continue to carry us on through.

FLEUR

Yes, time travel is the only way to continue.
I am determined to work out what happened, Carnation.
In my heart I know that Sherwin is in danger.

Maybe I can find some clues as to what has happened here.

CARNATION

Maybe.
Can you see him, Fleur?

FLEUR

Yes, I can.
I remember this moment, a day yesterday …

CARNATION

Go ahead and relive it, Fleur.
It might just help save us all.

FLEUR

Meeting you Sherwin,
outside the Fox Café in the early morning light.
Fresh picked daisies
smell fragrant in your hands.

Looking for the waitress, Celia.
Her beautiful nature still sparks
a radiant glow of light
through my muddy memories.

Celia is busily tending to a couple.
Her dark brown hair is windswept.
She still wears her outdoor jacket.

CELIA

Fleur, why are you here yesterday?
You've travelled alone, haven't you?

FLEUR

Maybe.

CELIA

It's obvious you have.
Sherwin is mute.
Can you hear anything he says?

FLEUR

No, I'm reliving a moment.
It's on autopilot.

CELIA

Give me your order quickly.
I'm running out of time.
There's someone I really need to find.

FLEUR

I understand, Celia.
I'll just order the usual thanks.

CELIA

Here's your order.
I'm running late now.
Let me crawl under your table, Fleur.
It's the safest exit.

FLEUR

Watching you replaying our chat, Sherwin.
Your gorgeous eyes are smiling.

CARNATION

Fleur, stay alert.

FLEUR

It's hard to.
Sherwin's here right now.

CARNATION

You mean he's present in the yesterday you're revisiting.
Concentrate on your routine.

FLEUR

I must.

Here I go…
Swirling warm, frothy milk in mugs,
savouring melted cheese on pizza.

Now we're ordering fine pastries
which we share together.
The chocolate filling is delicious.
Posing for final photos, I wait.

Leaving, you kiss me goodnight,
warming yourself in a long coat,
smiling as you walk out the door.

I stare after you, heart broken.
I wish that I could be with you.

By myself I wait even longer still,
running my fingers in table creases,
admiring the beautiful daisies.

DAISIES

You finally noticed us.

FLEUR

Yes, you are very beautiful.

DAISIES
We know.
Prolific too.
We are everywhere.

FLEUR
Is that so?

DAISIES
See if you can find more of us.

FLEUR
Sounds like fun!
Heading to the back of the café.
A young couple are slow dancing to soft music.
The girl is holding a daisy chain!
I've seen this image somewhere before…

DAISIES
You have.
Those daisies are fresh picked too,
just like we are,
to help you remember.

FLEUR
Where are you new daisies from?

DAISIES
The lawn out front.
We were picked yesterday.

FLEUR
By who?

DAISIES
You.

FLEUR
Me?

DAISIES
Speak to the Girl, Fleur.
She has the answers.

CARNATION

I wouldn't do that, Fleur.

FLEUR

Why not?
I can't see how it will hurt.
She might be able to help me.

CARNATION

Talking to her is a lure into another yesterday.
Don't you want to stay in this one?

FLEUR

I'm not sure.
I need to find him.

CARNATION

There are other ways.

FLEUR

I need to speak to her.
It's my decision to make.

Can I see your daisy chain, Girl?

GIRL

Sure.
Here it is, complete.
It's taken us both a long time to make this chain, Fleur.
The grass is sharp against my legs.
Can you help me up?

FLEUR

We're outside now.
It's dusk.
It's cold out here.

GIRL

Yes.
I should get my cardigan from the car.
Help me up?

FLEUR

Give me your hands.
Up you go.

FLEUR

This image of you is familiar,
the breeze blowing your hair
and lilac silk dress
as you struggle to keep standing.

GIRL

Can you see the stems in the air, Fleur?

FLEUR

Yes, they're rising and falling,
fighting to keep afloat.
Just like me.

GIRL

Grab one Fleur.
Examine it closely.

FLEUR

The stems are hard to grab.

GIRL

Try standing still, Fleur.
You need to stop running,
just for a moment ...
and watch.

FLEUR

I'm panting,
bending to catch a breath.

After a moment,
my breathing settles,
so does the breeze.
It is calm now,
still and silent.

The stems drop gently
over my head, face and arms.

Picking one up,
I take in its form.

FLEUR

It is green and wrought,
embellished with patterns
of fleeting lines ...
I wonder where they ...

A flash of memory hits me.
I am carrying a basket,
walking with the Girl,
across a meadow adorn
with blossoming daisies.

GIRL

What do you see Fleur?

FLEUR

We are picking flowers together.
Laughing.
You hand me some daisies.

GIRL

Yes I did.
A day yesterday in the meadow.
You've made some great
floral hair garlands with them Fleur.

FLEUR

I have?
For who?

GIRL

A couple of other girls and I.
It was important to you
that we ...
had them ready.

FLEUR

Ready? For what?

GIRL

You'll discover why soon.

FLEUR

I've had a memory.
It seemed very real.
It was brief ...

GIRL

A fleeting memory.
The stems will give you those.
They're right here in this yesterday,
for you to grab any time.

FLEUR

And so are you ...
I know you're important to me.

GIRL

This old memory of me is here.
A more recent memory may
be somewhere else.
You'll find me where you need to.
The stems will help guide you.

FLEUR

Thank you.
I wish I could remember your name.

GIRL

You will remember me one day,
when you are ready to.
There are still some stems on you.
They will travel with you.
Use them when you wish.

FLEUR

I will.
Thank you for helping me.

I've been so lost.

GIRL

Go now Fleur.
Tread gently
and keep watch.
Memories are precious.

FLEUR

I know.
I guess I'll ...
see you soon.

Act 1, Scene 3

CELIA
Under the picnic rug
are bursts of yellow and white.
Daisies lie waiting
to be part of my hairband,
which fits snugly on
Veronique's dark flowing hair.
How did it end up there?

The easel is wobbling
on top of a dinner plate,
which has remnants of
cake crumbs eaten for
yesterday's high tea.

Veronique is knitting a cardigan,
click clacking through blue -
the sky is very blue this yesterday.

I am so distracted,
stuck somewhere between
the earth and sky,
unsure where to set my eyes.

Spitter spatter goes the paint
I drop on ripped paper wrap,
which was used to wrap the -
mmm ... yummy fish and chips.
I can still taste them from -
lunch, which was, what day?
Yesterday, that's right.

The paint effect is, well, different.
It reminds me of jelly beans.
I could do with one of them right now.
I like the green ones best.
I just can't seem to focus today.

Veronique is always so focused.
Her knitting is amazing -
shop worthy.
You should start your own
knitting label Veronique.

CELIA

She is smiling at me,
a silent thanks.
That's Veronique, so humble.
Yet she never speaks …
Not to me, anyway.

The only way I get to see her
is to return to this yesterday.
She is always eternally knitting
that blue cardigan.

If I stand at different angles,
I get different views of Veronique.
Sometimes she is involved in intense
conversation with a mysterious other.
All she can do is replay what she did.
If only the present Veronique knew
how valuable she was in this past moment.

I know I'm a mess.
I haven't changed my clothes -
I'm embarrassed to say,
for two whole days.
My head is stuck in this aftermath.

I'll leave this setting as is,
it's momentous really,
marking the moments after -
it's too hard to think about that.
I can't even remember what day it was.
Tuesday, that's it, that afternoon.

Coffee stains smear the picnic rug.
There are still a few
lipstick-coated serviettes flapping
about in the breeze.
Here, then gone, people were.
Oh well.
At least I stayed after …
Poor Fleur.

I want to make one more mark,
now, after it all happened.
A memento of this yesterday.

CELIA

There, the picnic rug -
it looks great with paint drops,
like brand new.
I might still be able to use it.
It'll dry well in the sun.

My brain won't stop floating.
Don't laugh Veronique, please.
I need a sip of your tea,
I'm so thirsty.
Thanks, that's nice.
Is it raspberry tea?
Your nod is cute, Veronique.

Enjoy the sun, Veronique.
I know you'll be here
as long as it takes.
I left your glasses next to -
where did I ...?
That's right, the easel.
Silly brain, won't work.

Agapanthus, where are you?
I haven't lost you in this mayhem,
have I ...?

AGAPANTHUS

Can you see us, Celia?
More of us have risen from the grass
that your bare, searching feet have sunken into.
Steadfast and sturdy are we, *Agapanthus africanus*.
We have had to be, to survive since the seventeenth century.
Throughout time, we have been propagated around the globe.
We, *Albus Nanus*, are a renown cultivar,
who have adorned your world for a long time.

As flowers of love, we're here for you Celia,
ever since the moment you found us.
We see your confusion and pain
and will continue to accompany you
as you try to clear your mind.

CELIA

Wise Agapanthus, through your time,
you have witnessed much of life.
Such pain and torment you too would have felt,
along with me that very dark day.
Yet, still you stand, so gracefully,
confident and unafraid of any of it.
I see that your beautiful stalks and umbels
have bloomed into gorgeous, white,
trumpet shaped florets.

An honour it will be to have you
continue to accompany me.
After all that has happened, I will need your help
to locate and remember items and moments
that will help Fleur put the pieces
of her memories back together.
She so desires to remember the truth.

AGAPANTHUS

We'll do all we can to help you, Celia.
Do you know where you wish to begin?

CELIA

Yes. Let's crawl under the picnic rug.
Our quickest exit to the yesterday
when I began this painting.

Act 1, Scene 4

FLEUR

Red leaves drop
like charms across
the steep pathway.
It is autumn this yesterday.
My favourite maple tree
has begun shedding its leaves.

I hold onto the stem tightly,
pressing it thankfully against my cheek.
It has successfully landed me
here in this fleeting memory.

You, Sherwin, are standing under
the nearly bare branches,
leaning against the trunk.
Your brown eyes sparkle
with joy when they see me.
You take my breath away.

Your arms are strong around me,
drawing me in closely to your embrace.
Your warm, soft lips are so familiar against mine.

I miss you with all my heart.

What's that in your pocket?
It's bulky and square.
It's a small box.
I have it now, in my hand.
This box hides well in my pant pocket.

Yes, I will follow you,
holding your hand as we
venture across the pathway.

There is a faint rustling sound
through the trees,
a short distance away from us.

Ears pricked, I keep walking,
letting you lead me slowly
up the long pathway.

FLEUR

It twists and turns,
sandy gravel crunching
beneath my shoes.

Whoa!
You are pulling my hand firmly,
beginning to jog away from the sound.
I am keeping pace with you,
bursting into a faster run,
trying to escape the footsteps at our heels.

I just need to focus,
to stop and pay attention.

Time freezes as I turn.
I didn't know I could do that.
I can pause a fleeting memory?
What did I miss in this moment?
Let me see…

There stands a man in a blue sun hat,
frozen mid stride in his run.
His blue overalls cling tightly to his bare torso,
which glistens with droplets of sweat.

He looks angry.
Why?

CARNATION

Walk around and examine him, Fleur.
See what you can discover.

FLEUR

I can do that?
He won't chase me?

CARNATION

I don't believe he can move right now.
You have changed the natural course
of the fleeting memory.
You are now directing its course.

Now is your chance to discover some clues.

FLEUR

A dark shadow falls over the man's face.
His eyes almost swim in that shadow,
opening windows into a mysterious world.

I see that he desperately wants to reach us.
His outstretched arm ends with clawing fingers,
ready to snatch at something he desperately needs.
I know that it lies within the box I carry in my pocket.

Is that a pick hammer in his pocket?
I bet he dug deeply into the earth
with those grubby, slashed hands.
What was he destroying? Or hiding?

There is a rage burning within this man.
It dashes itself across the length of his arms
and his torso, which leans forward,
as though he is ready to pounce, to attack.

CARNATION

Perhaps he is, Fleur.
We both know that you've returned here for a reason.
Maybe this man has answers.

FLEUR

Yes, I've grabbed the object he desires.
Whatever it is, it has somehow
led to Sherwin's disappearance.
I need to know more.

CARNATION

Of course you do, Fleur.
Take a deep breath
and harness your inner strength.
You don't know what you will face.

FLEUR

Closing my eyes, I inhale,
calming my growing nerves.
This moment has taught me something valuable.
You are carrying a secret, Sherwin.

Opening my eyes, I look at your face.
Your expression is calm and accepting,
as though you expected to see this man.
You do not seem the least bit afraid.

FLEUR

How do you know him?
What happened for the man to be so angry?
Why is he is so desperate to take what you have?

We are so distant now, Sherwin.
You have a secret life
that consumes you, takes you away ...
Why?

You secret lies within this box.
I am going to open it.

The box is orange and leather.
I can hear something rustling inside it.
It opens so easily and
is very hollow, mostly empty,
except for...

Is that your mobile phone, Sherwin?
It's ringing so loudly in the silence.

There is a bright white light filling the space,
engulfing us all within its reach.
All I can see is a white emptiness,
swirling with an abundance of purple flowers.

CARNATION

What flowers are they Fleur?

FLEUR

I'm not sure Carnation.
Let me catch one.
This flower is such a deep purple colour.

CARNATION

Yes, it is.
How unusual. I've not seen this colour in the wild.

FLEUR

I can count many petals ...
there are around forty.
It has ten stamens in two whorls.
Its grey-green leaves are flat and linear, soft to touch.
Let me smell its fragrance.

CARNATION
Is it sweet?
Strong?

FLEUR
How odd.
This flower does not have a fragrance.

CARNATION
Very odd.
A flower with no scent is one to be wary of, Fleur.

FLEUR
Noted.

Are my eyes playing tricks on me or is the light flashing?

CARNATION
It is flashing, Fleur.
The wind seems to have picked up too.

FLEUR
We are rising, Carnation.
Hold on tight!

The wind is blowing with force now
and we are accelerating through the air at great speed.
The world zaps passed us like a whirlwind.

I land on hard wood planks, bouncing onto my bottom and thighs.
I am sprawled on my back,
staring up at the gold flowered handrail
of the footbridge ...

You are leaning on the handrail with one arm,
pulling fiercely at your hair.
A striking, handsome subject,
against a backdrop of the pink and purple hues of sunset.

Your phone is still ringing, intruding the
peaceful silence of the glowing sunset.
You look down at the caller identification
and shake your head with frustration.

Glancing over your shoulder, your eyes
are glazed over with worry.
You do not notice me lying on my back.

FLEUR

I can hear the shuffling of footsteps,
cutting across the gravel on the other side of the bridge.

You see him,
I do too.
The man in the overalls is approaching the bridge.
He has not seen you yet, as the dark
seems to have camouflaged you well.

There goes your jacket,
you've tossed it onto the ground.
Why did you do that Sherwin?
Do you want me to find it?
To know that you had left?

You are running now.
Your singlet clings tightly to your torso
and your muscles, well they are so strong,
so firm to touch …

I miss you so much…

You run clear of the bridge
and the setting around you changes.
The gravel beneath your feet
rapidly transforms into luscious,
soft green grassland.

You are disappearing again,
merging into the landscape of your chosen time.
Where did you go?

The other man's world is changing too.
The gravel is transforming into deep, brown dirt.
A dirt that is struck strongly with his hand pick
as he digs deeply, swiping the sweat away from his brow.
What is he looking for?

CARNATION

I don't know Fleur.
Whatever it is, it has consumed him.
He is fading now,
immersed in another time.

FLEUR

So here we are, Carnation.
Back to where it all began.
I wonder why the flower brought us here.

It is time to take a look inside the box.
It is a lovely orange colour,
vibrant and full of energy.
I can feel it pulse with life in my hands,
as though it has its very own heart beat.

The box has opened easily.
Yet, it appears to be empty.

CARNATION

Look closer, Fleur.
Sometimes things take a while to reveal themselves.

FLEUR

There it is!

It is a small vial
with a fine yellow dust inside it.

CARNATION

It looks vaguely familiar.
I know I've seen it somewhere before ...
Let me think ...

FLEUR

Whatever this is, Carnation,
it is powerful enough to make Sherwin run away
and vanish from life itself.

CARNATION

There is yellow dust on Sherwin's jacket, Fleur.

FLEUR

There is?
Let me see.

I can smell him, Carnation.

It is a reoccurring moment,
to slip his jacket onto me so easily again.
I feel like I am receiving a big, warm hug.

FLEUR

Maybe he's left something behind in one of the pockets.
These front ones are empty.
What about inside the lining?
Ah! He's had a secret pocket added.
There's something flat inside it.

It's a photo of Sherwin and I …
We are watering flowers upon a grassland.
I don't remember this moment.

CARNATION

I do.
I think I know what Sherwin is trying to tell you Fleur.

FLEUR

You do?

CARNATION

Yes, let's walk across the bridge, Fleur.
There's a place we should visit.
It might help give us some answers.

Act 1, Scene 5

CARNATION

Growth and senescence exists within me.
Each dawn, I am rejuvenated with the sun's glow
and with a fresh, new clove scent.
A scent that helps keep us both alert.

I feel safe upon Fleur's wrist
as she steps forward now,
her feet sinking into the fading grassland.
It has been cleared recently, I see.
Why?

My heart sinks when I think of the work
that both Fleur and Sherwin undertook
to give this grassland life, to nurture it.
Wild and free, we flowers were,
able to shoot meristem upon the hill grassland.

FLEUR

I wish I could remember what we did, Carnation.
I feel so out of touch.
Has everything changed?

CARNATION

Yes, it has.
Sherwin used to visit me here.
He would share stories of his time travels.
Yet one day, something in him changed, Fleur.

FLEUR

It did?
What happened Carnation?

CARNATION

His eyes darted wildly across the hill
and saw how it had begun to change.
A sense of panic filled his heart.

FLEUR

Did I notice the change too?

CARNATION

You did, Fleur.
The changes upset you.
You wanted answers.

FLEUR

I still do.

I feel a calling to take a few more steps further
and to glance at the hill of your past.
Would you be comfortable if I did that?

CARNATION

I can feel myself trembling, Fleur.
I know that I am about to feel immense pain
and that my view of the world will change.
I am terrified to bare witness to what lies ahead
and to accept a truth that I already know exists.

FLEUR

I can feel your fear, Carnation.
It reverberates through my body
and makes me stop short in my tracks.
Should we turn back?

CARNATION

Sometimes the hardest thing to do is the right one.
I couldn't live with myself if I turned back now.
Could you?

FLEUR

No, I couldn't either.
My mind may be muddy in its memories
but somehow, instinctively, I know I need to be here.
We have each other now, Carnation.
Whatever we see, we can face together.

CARNATION

Your strength is admirable, Fleur.
It sends a buzz of warmth through me,
reminds me that I am not alone.
I am lucky to be so cared for by you.

FLEUR

I also feel very cared for by you, Carnation.
I don't know what I'd do without you.

CARNATION

That is very sweet. Thank you.
Suddenly, I feel stronger than before,
knowing we will do this together.

I am ready now.

FLEUR

Alright.
I will walk slowly.
You tell me if you want me to stop, okay?

CARNATION

Okay.

The air feels colder suddenly,
I can feel it in bursts against my petals.
It sends a shiver through me.

FLEUR

I feel the chill too.
It is shooting across my arms,
making me tremble with cold.

CARNATION

It is so silent now,
so solemn.

FLEUR

We are here.

CARNATION

I see dirt, lots of it.
Look at the small rocks, which have become exposed
and jut out across the steepness of the hill.
There are so many small holes dug into the dirt ...
The other wild carnations are ...
gone.

FLEUR

My heart is breaking too.
The precious, wild carnations you speak of
must have been close to your heart.

CARNATION

They were, Fleur.
We, *Dianthus caryophyllus*
are sensitive to ethylene.
Our life span does not last too long
in our wild, natural state.

We all knew this, we wild carnations
and stood tall together, facing the forces of nature.
Each day was precious, feeling the wind kiss our petals
or the sun warm our very beings.

It is unusual though, Fleur,
that all the wild carnations are gone.
It was not long ago that I was with them
and some had only just sprouted.

I feel a deep ache inside me,
one that makes me feel as though
I should step into that darkness and let it cover me
like a thick, soothing blanket.
This reality is harsh and confronting,
leaving me feeling raw and alone.

FLEUR

I am here for you Carnation.
Can you feel me holding you tight?

CARNATION

There has to be something left, Fleur.
A petal, a carpel, anything that may
have propelled itself into that air.
Fought to breathe, to exist.
Please look closer.

FLEUR

Are you okay to ascend the hill?

CARNATION

Of course.
Be careful where you tread.

FLEUR

I will.

It is getting darker.
Should we look together?

CARNATION

More rocks, more holes.
Decayed grass.
Wait!

FLEUR

What is it?

CARNATION

It's a red petal, Fleur.
A wild carnation petal,
floating in the air.

FLEUR

So it is.

The petal is beautiful.
It has decided to land upon you.

CARNATION

I am happy to carry it with me, Fleur.
It may help relieve the deep ache I feel.

Am I the only wild carnation left, Fleur?

FLEUR

I believe so.

How lucky I am to have you with me, Carnation.
You are so naturally beautiful.
Look at your gorgeous sepals and pink petals, drifting lightly in the breeze.
I know that Sherwin would be so proud to see how much you have grown.

CARNATION

Thank you Fleur.
I am lucky to be with you too.
You are keeping me alive.
I know you'll do all you can to find the answers we seek.

FLEUR

Let's leave this place now.
It is too painful to stay.

CARNATION

Agreed.

FLEUR

It's time to grab a new stem, Carnation and see where it takes us.
Are you ready?

CARNATION

Yes.

FLEUR

Here we go!
I hope we land somewhere safe.

Act 1, Scene 6

CELIA

The shock has set in,
even after all this time has passed.
My eyes still don't want to settle,
leaving me stuck somewhere
between the earth and the sky.

You are my middle ground, canvas.
You may be blank, yet full of promise.
Maybe you can help me to see properly again.
My silly brain still won't work.

I get flashes of colour all the time.
For a start, I know that this blue streak I paint
was the colour of the sky that day.
I remember marvelling at its sheer crispness.

A cluster of flowers were visible across the meadow.
They were blue and what's that colour again?
White, that's right.

Beautiful, wild Agapanthus flowers, drew me into their space.
Amongst all the flames, that scorched our beloved meadow
and its hill, they still remained.
It still puzzles me why.

AGAPANTHUS

Our leaves are blessed with mucilage,
which is a water based gel.
It acts as a retardant and cools the fire.
That night, many of our leaves became black,
yet more sprouted rapidly from our rhizome,
rejuvenating us once more.

CELIA

You are so strong, Agapanthus,
my shining light of hope
in the never ending nightmares.
You were there to protect me.

I lay among you and ...
Hid.

CELIA

Shaking I was,
That's right, afraid.

Sparks of red and orange flew,
intruding violently upon
the wild's gentle peace.
Large, flickering flames
shot up high into the sky,
raging fiercely above me.

Where did I look?
Up or down?
Or somewhere in the middle ...?

My gaze is still transfixed there,
in that moment where I
faced the horror.

My memory shapes are distorted,
trying to realign themselves.
Silly brain, make sense of this.

Fleur once told me that breathing helps.
It feels good to stop and gently inhale ...
and exhale ....

That's better.
The shapes are clearing now.
No longer distorted, yet familiar.

I know that face.
My heart is pounding,
flooding with a swarm of emotion.
A face with a scar across
his right cheek.
Battle scar, he calls it.

A face that lures me closer,
draws me into its dark pools
of mystery and danger.
A face I wish I'd never met.

Act 1, Scene 7

FLEUR
I am catching the drift of wind,
my body floating lightly in the sky.
Somehow, this is familiar,
as though I have sailed
through the air before.

My arms are light and free
and my body is outstretched,
kissing the blue streaks.
I can breathe freely here.
It is soothing this moment,
an elation I treasure.

I am falling, slowly now,
dropping down to the earth.
Feet landing, I exhale a breath.
I am not afraid, yet rejuvenated.

The earth is soft and luscious,
adorned with dew kissed grass.
Kicking off my shoes,
I allow my bare feet to press
into the warm earth.
Dirt catches between my toes,
comforting me with its presence.

Staring up, my eyes fall upon an apex roof
atop a glass windowed building.
It is a glasshouse, structured with a steel frame.
I sense its warm glow, inviting me to step closer.

What is this building, Carnation?

CARNATION
A place you know well, Fleur.
You've spent a long time here.

FLEUR
I have?
There is something about these large windows
and the way they reflect the light
beaming from the sun.
It feels familiar to me.

FLEUR

I am intrigued by the front door.
Its steel framework swings in the breeze
and its glass glistens in day's light.

I am drawn to the entrance,
my bare feet pressing into the
crunchy, grey gravel pathway.

SHERWIN

What beauty stands in this room.

FLEUR

Is that Sherwin?
Do I turn around to see?
Or is his voice echoing
in my aching mind?

Sherwin?

SHERWIN

You feel so warm, Fleur.
I can feel your heart beat.
It's like a million butterfly wings,
giving life to my fleeting soul.

I wish I could ground myself
and hold you in my arms, Fleur.

FLEUR

I am drowning in a river of tears
that rip at my aching heart.
I can feel you Sherwin,
just within my reach.
How I long to touch you.

Can I face you?

SHERWIN

Best not to, my love.
You will not like the absence
and the stark nothingness.
Where you stand,
all is not as it seems.

FLEUR

This is not real, Sherwin?
These feelings we share?
You?
Are you a figment of my madness?
Have I finally lost my mind?

SHERWIN

You are very sane, Fleur,
in an unsettled world
that is trying to stop and rest.
Yesterday is yet to
catch up with the present.
It awaits a conclusion.

I am here with you, yet not,
reaching across the mad abyss
that seems to have ripped us apart.
We are stronger than this, though.
We will find our ways back
into each other's arms.

This moment, although fleeting
is very precious to my heart.
A moment I will not let go of,
yet hold onto tightly,
no matter how many moments pass.

FLEUR

Please stay a moment longer, my love.
Can you feel the precious intensity
of this moment?

Our hearts are real, Sherwin,
they continue to beat
even through buried time.

Deep in my own heart,
I will continue to wait for you, my love.
I will do all that I can to find you.

SHERWIN

The hunt begins here, Fleur.

FLEUR

It does?

SHERWIN

This place has many a time
and exists in many forms.
This was once our glasshouse,
our major conservation project.
We did all we could to
save the meadow's flora.
It has been unkept for
a long time, Fleur.

Local authorities have turned the other way
and allowed a commercial opportunist
to step in and seek his riches from our beloved meadow.

We both did all we could
to help the wild carnations, Fleur.
They had become highly sought after
by commercial flower breeders.

The carnations' pollens are sticky
and heavy in weight
and so are unable to be dispersed
through the wind's breeze.
This makes chances of natural
reproduction between carnations
very low in possibility.

We knew that this was the case
and grew cuttings of vegetation here,
which we transferred to parts
of the meadow and the hill,
so as to attract more
pollinators and encourage
vertical gene transfer between
the wild carnations.

FLEUR

Butterfly wings, in pastel colours,
still flutter in my mind.
I thought they were dreams,
now realise that they are memories
that have stayed with me
and so return to soothe me.

SHERWIN

Look around you, Fleur.
See the flowers that
you and I grew together here.

FLEUR

It brings me joy that we worked
for such a good cause, Sherwin.
We fought for nature's rights.

What beauty we created here.
Around me, bright colours bloom.
Big, swaying green leaves,
large growing beds
vibrant with the life of wild carnations,
daisies and agapanthus.
There are even some red roses …
soft petals that soothe my
troubled mind.

I remember now …
You, Sherwin, standing
amongst the rose beds,
smiling as you trimmed them.

Holding a rose cutting in your hand,
kneeling down on one knee
and placing it into my hands.

SHERWIN

Staring into your beautiful eyes,
adoring your radiant smile.

Asking you to be my wife.

FLEUR

I am shaking, now, as I feel
the love that we shared in that moment.
Our fervent promises to be together
for the life time that we would share.

Life is passing us by, Sherwin.

SHERWIN

It is simply letting us float, Fleur.
Time's magnets keep pulling us
back together, in the present or the past.

You must go now, Fleur,
danger lurks nearby.

FLEUR

What is it, Sherwin?

SHERWIN

Hide Fleur, quickly!

FLEUR

Sherwin?
Please don't leave me! I –

What don't you want me to see?

Gone is the beauty of
our beloved glasshouse.

The flowers and plants have wilted,
shrivelling away from
the rays of life.

Do I hear footsteps scuffing across the gravel?
It is hard to see behind this fern.
There is a tall man, entering the glasshouse.
His wild, dark hair flies out around his head.

His hands are piled with the earth.
Dirt he has dug up with his bare hands,
which drops in mounds across the gravel.

Dumping the remaining earth upon a table,
he stands, rifling through it,
pulling flowers recklessly from their life-giving soil.
Each rip is like a sharp knife,
slicing through my aching heart.

CARNATION

They are wild carnation flowers,
that once stood tall upon the hill.
Swaying gently in the breeze,
they basked in the sun's glow.

I hear their screams, Fleur.
They tear at my raging heart.
I wish I could stop this mad man.
He is heartlessly ripping them away
from their homes in the earth.

Their very lives lie in his hands.

JARONE

Hello *Dianthus Caryophyllus*,
there is a madness about you today.
Are you wiggling in my strong grasp?

Scattered and forgotten you were,
across the hill and its meadow.
Look at you in your wild state,
so unappealing to the commercial eye.

I need better, stronger carnations,
ones that will generate me wealth.
I can see you now, new and improved,
in flower shops and market stalls,
beloved by many across the globe.

You can and will be the talk
of every town, carnations.
A glamorous display for table tops,
in vases or even as a gifted bouquet.

CARNATION

His words bait me.
I feel a rush of anger inside me
and want to confront him.
How can he say this about my beautiful friends?

FLEUR

I'm sorry Carnation.
Hold back your anger and take stock of this moment.
Sherwin wants us to notice
something he believes is important ...

JARONE

It's great that Sherwin is away on holiday.
I can engage in secret work.
He has trusted me to care for the plants
and I will, not in the soft way he does.

For years I have trained in horticultural science.
Intra-specific breeding ...
Hybridisation and self pollination.
The way forward for the future
of better, cultivated flowers.

Now F1 generation of *Dianthus Caryophyllus*,
you'd be better as a new colour,
not this unattractive pink or red.
I'm thinking a deep purple colour,
it will certainly catch the eye.

As for your petals, well they
will certainly need to change.
Much too wild looking they are now.
Commercial carnations are special,
they need perfectly shaped petals.

Oh yes, your horrible scent,
we must rid of that clove smell.
Carnation flowers should not have a scent at all.
They should just be pretty
and last a long enough in a vase for someone to enjoy.

Stop wriggling in my fist!
You want to escape, don't you?
To return to your crazy wild state,
where your life is only short.

You don't know what's best for you.
I, Jarone, know what is best for you.
Yes I do.

CARNATION

Let me at him, Fleur!
I can't let him do this!

FLEUR

That is not a wise move, my dear, compassionate friend.
I cannot allow you to set yourself
upon this mad man.
We do not know what he is truly capable of.
I could not bear it if something happened to you.

CARNATION

I can't bear this Fleur.
It shakes me to my very core.
My dear, precious friends.

Help me, Fleur!

FLEUR

I've got you, Carnation.
Let me hold you tight.
You are safe with me,
I will take you far away
from this mad man.

I am sorry that Sherwin confronted you with this.
He left us both here to face the news all alone.
I wish I knew why.

There is only one person we can ask for direction now.

CARNATION

Who is that?

FLEUR

It's time to find my mother.

Act 1, Scene 8

CELIA

Fleur can't remember this gathering.
There are the plates, the cups, the serviettes …
marked with the prints of love and merriment.
So many came here, to this meadow,
to celebrate and be there for them both
that special day.

Distracted I was, by his dark eyes,
his promises that we would have time,
away from all this mayhem,
somewhere secluded and private.
A chance to be lost in each other.

Lured I was, into his desires.
Torn away from this gathering,
this precious, significant time.

Away from my duties for Fleur.

I keep returning to this moment,
it radiates like a beacon of light.
I know I am meant to discover
something important here.
No matter how much I trawl
through these remnants,
these marks of special presence,
I can't work out what it is.

AGAPANTHUS

Look straight ahead, Celia.
Can you see it, before your very eyes?
It is as white as we are,
hanging precariously over the edge of the table.

CELIA

I will try.

Yes, I see it.
It is falling to the ground
Scarred with burn holes and marks,
yet still it floats.
It whispers gently in the wind like Fleur with all her hope.

CELIA

There it lies, in a heap, on the ground.

I feel water running down my cheeks
and know that I am crying.
I am relieved to find this dress,
yet so sad at what it being here means.

There will come a time where Fleur
will be ready to see it, Agapanthus.
Not yet, though.
Until then, I will hide it somewhere safe.

Act 1, Scene 9

FLEUR

My village bell chimes the hour,
swinging away in harmony with the buzz of human life.
Vibrant red, green and purple
dresses float across the streets,
sharing their own special stories
with the busy streetscape today.

The dress I seek cannot be found.
It is tucked away deeply inside
the constant flickering shadows
of my very absent mind.
Images are blurry and blacked out,
unwilling to reveal their moments to me.

The hushed, heavily accented voice
comes to me again this yesterday.
It drifts through the breeze,
passed the market stands set up
along the side of the busy road.

I can't see her familiar face
standing behind the textile stall.

The stall is in fact empty,
void of the silk, cashmere and many
other beautiful materials that are sourced
from countries all around the world.

Her voice is like a comforting dream,
a lilting French hush, floating towards
me as I stand staring at the vacant display.

VERONIQUE

Fleur, te voilà.   (Fleur, there you are.)

FLEUR

Quel jour est-ce?   (What day is it?)

VERONIQUE

Le jour de la répétition.   (The day of the rehearsal.
Regardez ces œillets   Look at these carnations,
vous les portez dans un beau pot.   you carry them in a beautiful pot.
Des fleurs que tu as cultivées   Flowers you have nurtured
de tes mains aimantes, Fleur.   with your loving hands, Fleur.)

FLEUR

I have? I care for the carnations?

VERONIQUE

Oui, Fleur. Les œillets sur la colline   (Yes, Fleur. The carnations on the hill
disparaissent chaque jour.   are disappearing every day.
Savoir cela vous blesse   Knowing this hurts you deeply.)
profondément.

Toi et Sherwin faites tout ce que   (You and Sherwin are doing all you
vous pouvez pour les aider à   both can to help them survive.)
survivre.

FLEUR

Œillets d'hier.   (Carnations of yesterday.)

I remember them very clearly.
One early dawn I was frantic,
searching for wild carnations to save.
They were so fresh, a gorgeous pink.
My hands were trembling as I potted them.

They wilted considerably.
I searched the hill, the meadow,
trying to locate more, to save them.
They were … gone.

Only one carnation still thrived in the pot.
As the sun began to rise, its petals gleamed,
sparkling in the radiant light.
It was you, Carnation.

CARNATION

Me?

FLEUR

Yes, looking closer, I saw the water droplets across your petals.
They dripped into the dirt, like tears.
You were shaking, Carnation, distressed.

FLEUR

Your friends had left you behind.
You reached for me to help you,
to keep you alive.

You wrapped yourself around my wrist,
while the sun continued to rise.
I could smell your clove scent,
accompanying us as we journeyed into
the increasing brightness of day.
You've never left me, Carnation.

CARNATION

You have never left me, either.
I am so lucky to have you take care of me, Fleur.
Your memories may be muddied
but your caring nature is not.
Instinctively, you have always known
what needs to be done.

FLEUR

I knew how special the wild carnations were,
how they would help preserve our natural ways of life.

Sobbing, I left the departed carnations
lying in that meadow.
Somewhere, amongst all that grass.

I was running, as fast as I could,
carrying you, Carnation,
shaking and scared …

She was there, waiting for me.
Standing surrounded by a meadow of lavender,
her arms opened wide for me
to run into and cry and cry …

Maman, where are you now?
I need you to help me,
to tell me how to continue.
You'd know just the right thing to say.

VERONIQUE

I will speak in English, Fleur.
I am knitting something special.
I just need to complete the piece.
Soon I will see you again.

FLEUR
What are you knitting?

VERONIQUE
A surprise, you will see!
I know you will love it, Fleur.
It's your favourite colour.
You will need it for the cold,
while you go on your trek.

FLEUR
My trek?
I don't remember planning this.
Tell me more, Maman.
Who am I going with?

VERONIQUE
You and Sherwin both planned it Fleur.
You leave immediately after ...
Wait, what yesterday is it for you?

FLEUR
Sometime soon after everything happened.
I can't remember the day or the details.
I was hoping you could help me.

VERONIQUE
I'm sitting in the aftermath, Fleur,
still absorbing what happened.
I don't know every detail, just some.

FLEUR
Can I come and see you?
Can you tell me where you are?

VERONIQUE
Of course, darling Fleur.
You may not be ready to see everything just yet.

FLEUR
I will have to be.
I need to remember and understand.
It's the only way forward.

VERONIQUE

Is it?
Maybe it's time to let it go.
Start afresh.
Then we can all move on
and put this mess behind us.

Life is here to explore Fleur.
It is full of exciting new discoveries.
Embrace them.
Embrace the present.
Do not dwell in yesterday.

FLEUR

I need closure.
I need you, Maman.

VERONIQUE

I'll see you soon, Fleur.

FLEUR

Okay Carnation, it's time to help me go
back to the aftermath.
Do you know where that is?

CARNATION

I sure do.
Are you sure you are ready for this?

FLEUR

As ready as I'll ever be.

Ready Carnation?

CARNATION

If you're ready, then I am too.

FLEUR

Mmm. It is wonderful to breathe in
your special clove scent.

Time to close my eyes now.
I can see Maman's face
smiling warmly at me.

SUSAN MARSHALL

FLEUR

One more sniff of you Carnation.
Mmm ...

See? We are drifting backwards now,
heading towards ...
the aftermath.

Act 1, Scene 10

FLEUR

The atmosphere sears with a heat
that saturates my very being.
I am falling into a thick, smoky haze,
which racks at my lungs.

I sense an urgency ...
Outlines of bodies are
moving frantically through the space.

The onslaught of smoky fumes
smother the space below, entirely.
As the fumes billow through the air,
sparks of gold light flash from them.

The furnace of heat is overpowering ...
I cannot breathe.

How do I escape this?

Staring up, I watch gold sparks
alight and then drop, like fireworks,
exploding across the atmosphere.

Body parts shine in the light.
I can make out an arm, a leg,
two alarmed eyes of a person's face ...

What happened here?

People are climbing over each other,
desperately trying to escape.
As more gold sparks fall,
they scatter light across people's heads.
Mouths open wide, eyes close shut tightly.
Eyes open and stare straight into the distance ...

A scattering of shrill, frightened voices
echo across the space.
Language that is warped and non-sensical,
as though time has not caught up
with this very significant moment.

The people move faster, almost clawing at each other
as they desperately try to escape.

FLEUR

The mad, hysterical dashing has sped up,
creating quite a dizzy whirlwind.
Time jolts through this moment,
unsure where to settle.

Carnation?
Are you with me?

CARNATION

Yes Fleur, barely.
My scent can't survive these fumes.

FLEUR

No-one can.
We need to help these people escape.

CARNATION

A challenge, Fleur.
This is your aftermath.
You can control how it exists.

Look at what you've landed on.

FLEUR

I can barely see it through the haze.

Oh, it's a picnic rug.
It looks vaguely familiar.

CARNATION

Of course it does.
It's your mother's.

FLEUR

Yes, it is.
I can see the beautiful tassels that
she has attached to the sides of the rug.
She made it when I was very little.
It was a warm, comfortable blanket once.

Maman and I used to snuggle up on the couch together
with this blanket over our laps.
We would read my favourite stories together.

FLEUR

As I got older, we took the blanket on outings with us.
I always felt much calmer and safer when I held it.
I realise now that it was my security blanket.
In some ways it still is, landing me here safely.

CARNATION

It is still your security blanket now, Fleur.

FLEUR

Yes it is, Carnation.

I have an idea.
I will take this blanket with me,
tossed over my shoulder like this.

CARNATION

You can do it, Fleur.

FLEUR

Yes, I can!

Stepping forward determinedly,
lured by the mesmerising haze,
feeling the fiery rage of its heat.

Heaving the blanket with all my might,
smothering the giant fumes.
It is hard work, jumping up high
to face the swarm of fumes head on.

My eyes are stinging!
I can't breathe!

Pushing passed the pain, battling on.

How much time has passed?
I am so fatigued.

I must save this situation.

The fumes are extinguishing.
There is the welcome, natural light of the sky.

The danger is passing, Carnation.
Can you see the people's panic subsiding?
They are dropping to the ground or
stopping to catch a grateful breath of clearer air.

CARNATION
Well done, Fleur.
It seems that you have tamed the aftermath for now.

FLEUR
Yes, for now.
I am so thankful to breathe in clearer air, Carnation.

CARNATION
Yes, what a relief.

FLEUR
I see many plates of cake slices
scattered across the lush, tall green grass.

Filled and half empty cups of tea lie tipped or standing,
some marked with lipstick stains from drinking.
A celebration took place here.

Some people are sitting, returning to their meal,
smiling and chatting among themselves as though the previous,
devastating moment never occurred.

CARNATION
You have more control over time than you realise, Fleur.

FLEUR
Yes, it seems I do.
I still need answers though, Carnation.

CARNATION
Patience Fleur.
You will have your answers in good time.

FLEUR
It's nice to see that the people have settled down now.

CARNATION
They've returned to replay this celebration.
It's all they can do in this moment.
We shouldn't stay too much longer, Fleur.
It's best that you do not become stuck in this yesterday.

FLEUR

There stands a solo figure.
Her long, dark hair is parted into a bun
with loose strands falling across her eyes.
Her figure is very warm and familiar to me.
Her light, French hush drifts through the air,
filling the space like a warm, comforting hug.

VERONIQUE

Te voilà, ma chérie Fleur.   (Here you are, my darling Fleur.
Votre force de volonté et de   Your strength of will and
détermination ne vous a pas quittée.   determination has not left you.)

Je vois que vous avez réglé   (I see you settled down
la brume des conséquences.   the haze of the aftermath.
Vous seul pouvez le faire.   Only you can do that.)

FLEUR

Maman!
Ma force vient de toi et de   (My strength comes from you
tout ce que tu m'as appris.   and all you taught me.)

VERONIQUE

Il faut parler Français, Fleur.   (We must speak French, Fleur.
Il reste encore du travail à faire.   There is still more work to do.
Une force maléfique est en jeu ici,   An evil force is at play here,
celui qui brûle comme le feu.   one that burns like fire.
Nous devons trouver   We need to find its source
sa source et l'exposer.   and expose it.)

FLEUR

Bien sûr Maman.   (Of course Maman.
Je ferai tout mon possible   I will do all I can
pour trouver mon amour ...   to find my love ...)

VERONIQUE

Alors tu devrais, Fleur.   (So you should, Fleur.
Il aura besoin de votre aide.   He will need your help.)

FLEUR

Je veux te faire un câlin, Maman.   (I want to hug you, Maman.)

VERONIQUE

Ne m'approche pas, Fleur.
Nous attirerons l'attention
indésirable sur nous-mêmes.
Vous ne savez jamais
qui nous regarde.

(Do not approach me, Fleur.
We will draw unwanted attention
to ourselves.
You never know
who is watching us.)

FLEUR

Très bien maman.
Au moins je peux te voir tricoter.
Tu me manques tellement.

(Alright Maman.
At least I can see you knitting.
I miss you so much.)

VERONIQUE

J'ai besoin de votre aide pour me
libérer des conséquences, Fleur.
Ferez-vous ce que je vous demande?

(I need your help to
release me from the aftermath, Fleur.
Will you do as I ask?)

FLEUR

Bien sûr Maman.
Je ferai ce que vous voudrez.

(Of course Maman.
I will do as you wish.)

VERONIQUE

Je me tiendrai dans un instant
et rejouerai une conversation
que j'ai eue à cette fête.

(I will stand in a moment
and replay a conversation
I had at this party.)

Pendant mon absence, j'ai besoin
que vous récupériez ce cardigan fini.
C'est pour toi, Fleur.
Une fois que vous l'aurez mis,
vous me libérerez de ce terrible
moment.

(While I am gone, I need you
to collect this finished cardigan.
It is for you, Fleur.
Once you put it on,
you will release me from this terrible
moment.)

FLEUR

Où iras-tu?

(Where will you go?)

VERONIQUE

Partout où le temps me laisse aller.
Espérons que quelque part
dans le présent.
Plus tôt nous réglerons
ce désordre, mieux ce sera, Fleur.

(Wherever time lets me go.
Hopefully somewhere
in the present.
The sooner that we sort
out this mess, the better, Fleur.)

J'aimerais retrouver ma
vie de tous les jours.

(I would like my
everyday life back.)

FLEUR

Moi aussi.	(Me too.
Sherwin aussi, s'il le pouvait.	So would Sherwin, if he could.)

VERONIQUE

Êtes-vous prêt Fleur?	(Are you ready Fleur?)

FLEUR

Oui.	(Yes.
Prends garde, maman.	Take care, Maman.)

VERONIQUE

Toi aussi, chérie Fleur.	(You too, darling Fleur.
Laisse-moi te jeter un dernier regard,	Let me take one last look at you,
avant que je parte.	before I go.)
Puissions-nous nous revoir	(May we see each other again
très bientôt.	very soon.)

FLEUR

Maman is approaching a middle-aged woman,
who is eating a slice of cake.
The woman has black smudges of smoky ash
smeared across her face and red hair,
remnants of the terrifying moment
that we have managed to escape.

I too must be covered in black ash.
It would help to conceal my face and
hide me away from observant eyes.
I can feel many eyes on me now
as I travel across the space.

Adjusting the blanket over my shoulder,
I keep my eyes peeled straight ahead.
I can hear the faint whispers of my name.
People are beginning to recognise me.
I need to move quickly now.

Approaching where Maman once sat,
my eyes fall upon a heap of cerulean blue material.
The blue of the sky, my favourite colour.
Bending down, I snatch up the material
and shake it loose with my left hand.

FLEUR

It is a gorgeous, blue cardigan,
knitted with the shapes of the autumn leaves
that Sherwin and I discovered on our walks together.
Leaves we would lovingly collect and hang on display.
Some nights we would fall asleep together under the leaves,
listening to the strong, loving beats of each other's hearts.

I can hear my name loudly now.
A few people are waving at me to approach them.
I will need to work quickly before
I am dragged further into the aftermath.

The cardigan feels warm and comfortable on my cooling arms.
I button it up and run my hands gently over its
beautiful autumn leaves …

I will revisit you again very soon.

VERONIQUE

What a radiant, golden light,
shining like an early morning sunrise.
It is so warm and inviting,
let me take a step into it.

Wow! Is that my market stall?
I can see it there.
It's not too far away.
Let me reach you …

FLEUR

Heads turn to stare at me,
their eyes are frightening, full of questions.
A few people are stepping closer, advancing towards me.
I have seconds to escape.
Who knows what will happen to me here?

It's time to go, Carnation.

CARNATION

I'm sorry Fleur.
My scent has completely faded after the smoke.
I can't help you now.

FLEUR

It's okay, Carnation.
We will have to find another way.

CARNATION

Think fast, Fleur.
They are nearly upon us!

FLEUR

There must be a way out of here …

If I close my eyes,
I might just be able to block out
this interference.

I can see the Girl's face again,
smiling at me.
She is wearing the lilac dress
and is carrying the daisies.

GIRL

Here I am, Fleur.
What a dark, eerie moment in time.
Where are we?

FLEUR

In the aftermath.

GIRL

I see that you are in danger.

FLEUR

Yes, I am.
I need to escape.

GIRL

Close your eyes, Fleur, relax.
You know the memory that you wish to return to.
Picture it now in your mind.

FLEUR

I can't.
I'm afraid.

GIRL

Ignore the people, Fleur.
You can control this moment more than you realise.
Be positive.
Think of your love for Sherwin.

FLEUR

I am closing my eyes.

I can see a precious body of water,
glistening in the dappled light.
There it is, the beautiful village lake!

GIRL

Good.
Keep your eyes closed,
ignore this very moment.
It does not need your attention.

Now, grab your stem Fleur.
That's it, hold it tight.

Let your mind remember what you did
that day on the lake...

FLEUR

I remember ...

I can feel my body rising into the air
as the stem takes me away from the dark, lingering aftermath.
I am heading towards a romantic moment at our village lake,
where I peered into the deep, blue eyes
of my love, Sherwin...

Act 2, Scene 1

FLEUR

Golden, red and russet leaves fall gently
across the bank of our small village lake.
It is autumn this yesterday, the last season
I spent with my love, Sherwin.

The autumn leaves remind me of my own faded memories.
The leaves hold their own precious stories,
which drift about in the wind,
finding a new place to settle
and continue to exist.

The bare branches of the elm tree
still stand tall and strong, like I do.
It is a reminder that life still continues
even during the most adverse times.

As I land gently on the grassy plain,
my attention is drawn to the sight of fallen autumn leaves,
floating across the steady stream of water.

Sherwin has presented me with
many of these beautiful leaves in the past.
They are symbols of our steadfast endurance as a couple
and bring warmth and joy to my heart.

The fallen leaves gather at the side
of the bank that I have landed upon.
Rolling into a sitting position,
I take in their beautiful, delicate forms.
They are a gift to me on this special day.

Crawling across the grassy terrain,
I reach out with my left arm
and retrieve the leaves from the water.
They are beautiful shades of green, red, orange and gold.

Sitting again, I hold the leaves close to my chest
and breathe in their beautiful, comforting scent.
I feel soothed, my mind leaving the traumas
of the aftermath in the distance,
ready to face a more positive day.

I know this yesterday, I remember it fondly.

FLEUR

It is the anniversary of our engagement.
Sherwin and I visited our favourite lake
to spend some quality time alone together.

The elm tree's leaves sway gently
in the calm, soothing breeze.
I can feel Sherwin's beautiful, gentle presence.
A small whisper echoes around me.

SHERWIN

I see you, my beautiful Fleur,
as gentle and precious as the leaves you clasp.
My love, I want nothing more than to hold you.

FLEUR

You can, Sherwin.
Lift me up into your breeze.
I will float with you.

SHERWIN

I'll see what I can do, Fleur.

FLEUR

It is silent for a while,
as the wind begins to gradually build.
The elm leaves flutter more strongly now,
many falling and scattering across the lake.
I can feel some landing upon my hair and my cheek.

Is that you, Sherwin?

SHERWIN

Yes, it is Fleur.
It's nice to feel your soft hair and skin.
Close your eyes.

FLEUR

Closing my eyes, I let myself relax.
I feel safer knowing that Sherwin is with me.
I trust him with my heart and soul.

I can feel my body slowly rising.
A gentle gust of wind blows against my back
as I rise higher and higher into the air.

SHERWIN

Open your eyes now, my beautiful Fleur.

FLEUR

Those gorgeous blue eyes,
wide and smiling at me with joy.
Sherwin!

SHERWIN

Try not to speak, Fleur,
It takes a lot for me to focus
and reveal my whole self to you.
It's so cold where I am.

FLEUR

Cold?
Are you shivering?

SHERWIN

Yes, I am.
I've been here for a while Fleur,
wading in the water.
I don't know how much longer I can last.
Sometimes I think the day is going
to swallow me in its vapour of ash.

FLEUR

Where are you, my love?

SHERWIN

In our own aftermath, Fleur.

FLEUR

Where is that?

SHERWIN

At this very lake.
You don't remember, do you?

FLEUR

No.
I don't think I'm ready to yet.

SHERWIN

Your memory will return when it's ready.
I haven't got much more energy, Fleur.
The wind is helping me to time travel
and be here with you this yesterday.
If I talk too much,
I will break our connect -

FLEUR

Shh … enough said.
Your lovely hair, so golden and soft …

SHERWIN

Your beautiful face, your soft skin …

FLEUR

Let me kiss you, Sherwin.

SHERWIN

I would love that.

FLEUR

My love, if all we have is this moment,
then let it be one where we love freely …

SHERWIN

I love your warmth.

FLEUR

Yours too.

Please stay with me.

SHERWIN

You know that I can't, Fleur.

FLEUR

Are you in great danger?

Sherwin, answer me.

SHERWIN

I don't think I can wade for much longer, Fleur.
My arms are so tired.

Let me spend these last fleeting moments with you
before I completely run out of energy.
It feels so good to hold you
and feel your touch again, my love.

FLEUR

Hold me close, Sherwin,
as tightly as you can.
Let our bodies beat as one
until the sun falls over this lake.
This may heal our fragile hearts,
deeply in need of each other's love.

Act 2, Scene 2

FLEUR

The sun is rising gently this morning,
flickering its precious lights of life.
I can feel your arms around me,
hear your soft breathing in my ear.

Some moments I want to cling to,
hold on tightly too and never let go of.
Moments like these where my heart
soars with the euphoric feeling of love.

SHERWIN

Are you awake, Fleur?

FLEUR

Yes.

SHERWIN

It's beautiful, the sunrise, isn't it?

Fleur?

FLEUR

Bittersweet.
I don't want you to go.

SHERWIN

Let me drop you off somewhere.

FLEUR

Really?
Where?

SHERWIN

Where would you like to go?

FLEUR

To a moment we've both experienced.
It will help me to remember.

SHERWIN

Are you sure you're ready for that, Fleur?

FLEUR
Yes.

SHERWIN
Okay, I'll take you there.
First, let's chase these leaves
floating through the air.
A game we used to play.

FLEUR
Help me remember.

SHERWIN
Take my hand.

FLEUR
Are we flying?

SHERWIN
Yes.

Catch a leaf Fleur, it may trigger a memory.

FLEUR
This is challenging!

SHERWIN
Keep trying.
You've always been so good at catching them.

FLEUR
I have?
Wow! I caught one!

SHERWIN
Well done!
Just float, Fleur,
close your eyes and let your mind be.

FLEUR
I can see so many images.
I see Maman helping me put on a dress.
The dress is white and long,
it is very beautiful.
Maman is taking my measurements,
making sure she can fit it correctly.

FLEUR

I feel a sense of lightness in this dream,
as though I am very happy, excited.
Sherwin, did you see me in the dress?

SHERWIN

Yes Fleur,
but not as it was planned.

I would have loved to have seen you the way we wished,
to hold your hands when you arrived.

FLEUR

When I arrived?
Where?

SHERWIN

On the hill, Fleur,
adorned with the colourful carnations that we love.

FLEUR

The village hill?
At times, when I have the confidence to face the present,
I return to the hill.
I know an important memory lies there.

SHERWIN

It does.
It is our memory, Fleur.

FLEUR

It is?
I've seen the hill's ashes,
they float through the air
and sprawl across the barren dirt
of the connecting meadow.

SHERWIN

I can still see them now, Fleur.

FLEUR

You can?
How sad.
There was life there once,
I feel so sad that it's gone.

SHERWIN

Not gone, Fleur,
just resting for a while.
That meadow and its hill still have many stories left to share.

Do you still have the vial, Fleur?

FLEUR

The vial?
Yes, it's in my pocket.

Here it is.

SHERWIN

Keep it well hidden.
Do not open the vial as it holds the key to renewal.
Inside that vial is a very powerful mix of pollens,
which once released,
can take you to a moment in time that your heart desires.

FLEUR

How did you get this pollen?

SHERWIN

One twilight, as the sun was falling,
I was floating through the wind,
time travelling with Jarone.

You remember him, Fleur?

FLEUR

I'm not sure.
Who is he?

SHERWIN

Jarone was a friend I met time travelling.
He took an interest in my pursuits.
We travelled together for a while,
completing many missions together.

FLEUR

What does he look like?

SHERWIN

He has dark hair and likes to wear a baseball cap.

FLEUR
A baseball cap.

I saw him recently, when you left me in the glasshouse.

I had to face a truth that I was unprepared for.

SHERWIN
I'm sorry, Fleur.
Jarone is dangerous.
Stay clear of him.
He wants the vial that you carry.

FLEUR
Right.
Is the pollen important?

SHERWIN
Yes, it is very special.
I found it that particular day,
time travelling with Jarone.

At first I noticed a small, yellow speck
floating in the breeze.
Picking it up, I held it between my
thumb and forefinger, admiring its beauty.
Suddenly, my heart felt a strong pull,
a desire to return to your arms.

I landed in that yesterday,
holding you close on the couch,
staring deeply into your eyes.
I'll never forget the joy in your eyes,
the excited catch in your voice,
at having me there beside you.

FLEUR
The pollen gave you your desire?

SHERWIN
Yes and more.
I saw the vibrant, beautiful complexity of you in that moment.
The continuation of our lives and love together.

FLEUR
Jarone knows about the pollen's power?

SHERWIN

Yes, he does.
He will do anything to get it, Fleur.
Anything.

FLEUR

Do you think he's responsible for the fire?

SHERWIN

Very possibly.
Jarone is very dark.
His travels are private and somewhat violent.
He always returns with battle scars.
He's not afraid to attack.

FLEUR

I understand.
To think he could have burned our hill and our meadow.
I hate to think of anything worse that could have happened …

SHERWIN

Yes, I know.
When the fire began that night,
I looked everywhere for you, Fleur.
You were gone.

As I rose up to the sky, my heart was broken.
I let the wind carry me, tears streaming down my cheeks.
I could see the pollens of the flowers and trees
releasing themselves into the air.
Lifting up my shirt, I caught as much pollen as I could.
Anything to save my time with you.

FLEUR

How do I reach you, my love?
You are here, yet so far away.

SHERWIN

Step away from yesterday, Fleur.
Allow yourself to become actively
aware of the present.
This may mean letting me go.
However difficult that may be.

FLEUR

I can't let you go, Sherwin!
Do not ask that of me!

Nor can I let go of our yesterdays.
It's the only way that I can still see you.

SHERWIN

Time has a way of revealing stories.
Our story drifts in the eternity
of unravelling moments in time.
Hours, days and weeks will continue to pass,
carrying our forms through the air,
letting our stories hang in the gentle breeze.
Our love will always be here,
reaching out through gusts of wind,
to clasp us in its secure embrace.

I need to let you fall now, Fleur,
gently back to the ground.
Allow yourself to feel the solid world beneath your feet.
See the world for all it displays, no matter how microcosmic.
Let yourself live, my love.

FLEUR

No, Sherwin,
please don't leave me.

SHERWIN

I have to, Fleur.
It's not good for you to remain in this state for too long.
You will lose track of the present time and travel the world aimlessly.

Keep yourself grounded, Fleur,
you need all your strength to find me.

FLEUR

I will try, Sherwin.
Thank you for such a precious time.
I miss you so much.

SHERWIN

I miss you too, Fleur.

I can't hold out much longer.

FLEUR

I promise you, I will find you.

Please take care, my love,
we'll be together again soon.

Act 2, Scene 3

FLEUR

I am falling,
staring up at the universe.
A myriad of colours swirl, making my head spin.
What are these microcosmic, black particles?

CARNATION

I'm not sure, Fleur.
They have a scary feel about them.

ASH

Rising,
floating
Ash.

FLEUR

What eerie, distorted voices.
We are surrounded by a nightmare.

ASH

See what we are, Fleur.
Follow us.
Rising,
floating
Ash.

FLEUR

Like insects, the ash is pooling around us,
drawing us close, pushing us further down.
Help me swipe at the shapes, Carnation!

Stand back!

ASH

Stand back?
Fire does not stand back!
It rages on and on!

At first we liked the warmth,
the way it flickered in the wind.
So bright and intoxicating.

ASH

Now we are left cold,
rising ...
floating ...
Searching for a new source of heat.
We are all that is left.

FLEUR

All that is left of what?

ASH

Mad desire, Fleur.
Greed.
Blood fire rages afterward.
It's time you faced it ...
Burnt out, monochrome.

FLEUR

I am descending rapidly.
The skies are a crazy, swirly blur.
The ash particles grow thicker
and a chill shoots down my spine
as I reach the very present ground.

Ouch!
My bottom!
I am dazed.

My vision is beginning to clear.
I see that I have landed in dirt.
Bare, barren dirt with the scars of fire.

ASH

Watch Fleur.
See the world as it is ...

FLEUR

The land is slowly changing.
Hues are disappearing, leaving
a dark tint over the land and grass.

ASH

This is the soul of your aftermath, Fleur.
Its vital pulse.
What do you see?

FLEUR

Barren land,
broken trees.
Bones, lots of bones.
A man standing with his back to me.
He is wearing a baseball cap.

Jarone!

ASH

Grab his attention, Fleur.

FLEUR

I will not.

ASH

Follow your desires, Fleur.
He has a message for you.

FLEUR

Carnation, are you here?

CARNATION

Yes, Fleur.
I'm here.

My scent is weak.
The fumes of smoke overpower it.

FLEUR

What do we do?

CARNATION

Freeze time, Fleur.
You know you can.
You've done it before.

ASH

Face the man, Fleur.
All will be okay.
He will give you what you need.

FLEUR

I choose to walk away from the Ash,
away from Jarone.

ASH
You might slow us down
but we will fight back!

FLEUR
Standing still, I wait.
The Ash stops moving.
So does Jarone.

CARNATION
Well done, Fleur,
you have succeeded.
Do you want to see the secret?

FLEUR
I do.

CARNATION
Walk backwards towards him.
If you walk forwards, you will restart time.

FLEUR
I can't see where I am walking, Carnation.
Can you guide me?

CARNATION
Keep walking straight.
Now step to your right a little.
One more step and you are facing him Fleur.
Are you ready?

FLEUR
I have to be.
Time is running out, Carnation.
If I even have a chance at saving Sherwin…

CARNATION
Say no more, Fleur.
Focus.

FLEUR
Eyes closed, I take a deep breath.
All will be fine.
One last step.

FLEUR

He can't move, only I can.
Do this for yourself, for your loved ones.
For Sherwin.

I dare to open my eyes and look at Jarone.
His eyes are the colour of red fire,
burning strongly, like the depths of hell.

He has a twisted, tormented smile on his face.
In his hands, he holds a bunch of dead carnations.

Sherwin and my special flowers,
dead and decaying, right there in his hands,
along with a bent, tattered photo.

Taking the photo from his hand,
I open it up, staring at the very confronting image.
It is of me, in a long, white dress, picking daisies.

The burning, tormented Jarone
with a heart that is twisted and torn.
A man who is hunting me down.

CARNATION

Move quickly now, Fleur.
Time is catching up.
The Ash is beginning to move again.

FLEUR

Pocketing my photo, I muster my courage.
Sherwin has asked me to face this present time,
no matter how hard it is.
Face it, I will!

Hold tight, Carnation!

I run as fast as I can,
across the burnt dirt and into the forest of elm trees.
Mere skeletons they are now,
marked with the scars of fire.

I can hear the stomping of footsteps, not too far behind me.
Jarone has awoken,
it won't be too long until he finds me.

Regal Elm,
Regal Elm,
open your home!

FLEUR

My throat is burning as I whisper,
the stench of smoke fumes making me gag.
I can feel water building up in my eyes.
Tears begin to roll down my cheeks.
I cough and splutter, gasping for air.
It is hard to breathe.

ELM

I hear you, beautiful Fleur.
I am glad you have returned.
Nature needs your help.

FLEUR

Let me in!
Let me in!

ELM

What are the secret words, Fleur?

FLEUR

Really?
You want me to remember?

ELM

You shouldn't have forgotten, Fleur.
You've known me since you were a child.

FLEUR

You know who I am.

ELM

How do I know you're not an imposter?
You're in danger, aren't you?

FLEUR

Yes, listen.
Jarone has nearly caught up with me.
He is very dangerous.
Please help me to hide for tonight.

ELM

Of course.
First, the secret words.

FLEUR

Okay!
At least I do remember these words: *vrai cœur*.

ELM

Come inside, Fleur. Quickly!

FLEUR

Thank you Elm.
You have saved me.
I will be eternally grateful.

It's warm inside your tree hollow.
I see you still have my dried leaf bed set up in here.

ELM

Of course.
It is ready for you to use at any time.

FLEUR

How sweet.
I am so tired.
This bed is still so comfortable.
Am I drifting off to sleep, Carnation?

CARNATION

Yes, you are.
Sleep all you need, Fleur.

FLEUR

Is the hollow door shut?

ELM

Yes, it is locked.
No-one can enter.

FLEUR

Then I might sleep.

CARNATION

Sleep as much as you can, Fleur.
We both need to recharge before we face
tomorrow and its aftermath.

FLEUR
Goodnight Carnation,
sleep well.

CARNATION
May your sleep be blessed with sweet dreams, Fleur.

Act 2, Scene 4

FLEUR

Early day's rays shine,
awakening the world.
I rise with the light,
lifting myself off the ground.

I stretch towards the skies.
If I stand still I can feel the slightest,
ever so calmest ... breeze.

I breathe, 2, 3, 4,
letting myself drift.
My arms raise, my breathing regulates.
I float into the breeze.

The air is lulling, caressing
like a soothing blanket.
My heart aches with gentle memories
of time shared with Sherwin.

The breeze gently releases me.
I am landing on top of the barren hill.
There is my mother's market stall.

VERONIQUE

Fleur, te voilà.   (There you are Fleur.)

FLEUR

Quel jour est-ce Maman?   (What day is it Maman?)

VERONIQUE

Le jour de la marché   (Market day.
Regardez ces œillets violets,   Look at these purple carnations,
Ne sont-ils pas beaux?   aren't they beautiful?)

FLEUR

Non ils ne sont pas.   (No, they are not.

Ils ne sont pas naturels, Maman.   (They are not natural, Maman.)

VERONIQUE

Qu'est-ce qui te fait dire ça, Fleur?   (What makes you say that, Fleur?)

FLEUR

I will speak English, Maman.
It is a truth that Sherwin shared with me, not too long ago.
It seems yesterday is changing drastically, Maman.
Our meadow is being destroyed for commercial desires.

The carnations at your stall are not the wild ones of our hearts.
They are hybrid carnations,
grown so that they can sell well on the market.
You would not believe the lengths a plant breeder
will go to in order to rid a carnation of its undesired traits
or to create a perfect petal or to obtain a bigger sized flower ...

VERONIQUE

This is not right, Fleur.
It makes me livid.
Do we know who is doing this?

FLEUR

Yes, we do.
He has a dark soul and a secret desire.

VERONIQUE

What is his name?

FLEUR

Jarone.

VERONIQUE

Oh, Jarone Wilker.
I know the man.
He ventured into our town just a couple of years ago, Fleur.
He was troubled and solitary.
He did not speak to many.
There was a madness about him, that was obvious.

We always wondered if he had something to do with ...

FLEUR

With what, Maman?
Tell me.

VERONIQUE

With the tragic events that occurred.
With your loss of memory.
He seemed to disappear around that time
as mysteriously as he arrived.

You have a skill, Fleur.
One that may just help save this meadow.
I am hoping that being here may just help you to remember.

FLEUR

I do?

VERONIQUE

Oui.   (Yes.)
Look closely at the ground, Fleur.
It will help you to rediscover your heart.

FLEUR

Where will you be, Maman?

VERONIQUE

The only place I can be,
this version of my market stall in the aftermath.
I miss my beautiful material.

Travel safe, my darling Fleur.
Button up your cardigan to keep you warm.

FLEUR

I will, Maman.
See you soon.

My heart falls as I see
a ground absent of flora.
Such beautiful flowers used to adorn this meadow and its hill.
It is the place where I fell in love with Sherwin.

I remember now,
we were lying, right here,
on this very patch of –

I can feel tears falling from my eyes.
It is so incredibly sad, this situation.

CARNATION
Yes, it is Fleur. Very sad.
The meadow and its hill are now a graveyard.

FLEUR
Agreed, Carnation.

Closing my eyes, I listen to the silence.
It is a moment to connect with nature.
I bathe once more in the calm blue skies: 2, 3, 4,
soaking in the radiant light rays: 4, 5, 6.

Warmth radiates from my skin.
I breathe in: 2, 3, 4 ...
Expelling my energy: 4, 5, 6,
feeding the substrate of the hill and its meadow.

The life oppressed hill creaks,
beginning to tremor beneath my feet.
I breathe in: 2, 3, 4,
trying to maintain the warmth.

Its substrate begins to burst with buds,
small, green buds that, given warmth,
accelerate rapidly in growth,
until my warmth is not needed anymore.

Standing back, I accept the echoes
of gratitude from the awakened hill.
Looking down, I await the guidance
it has rewarded me with.

Lush and green, it is life
that Maman and I know existed here once before.

VERONIQUE
My darling Fleur,
you've rediscovered your skill.
Keep going, use it wisely!
You'll save our meadow!

FLEUR
A beautiful miracle is unfolding.
Life has awoken in its green finery.
So welcome in our arid, burnt world.

GRASS

Stark against the bright light,
we grass stems unfurl our blades.
Voices whisper beneath our green,
a time past of painful silence.

The voices build to a loud roar,
distorted and inconsolable.
Our new life feels remorse
for this world's painful loss.

We brace our stems, ready to defend
the right for nature to exist.

FLEUR

Time to move.
I inhale a deep breath: 1, 2, 3 …
and breathe a breeze upon the grass: 4, 5, 6.

GRASS

The gentle breeze sets us in motion,
sprouting across the earth.
Following footprints, we sprawl down the slope of the hill
and across the barren meadow.

FLEUR

Still I breathe in, focusing my mind on
the pathway taken by the grass blades.
I stand on the meadow now,
the temperature is becoming hotter here.
A flash of red light breaks my focus.

I bare witness to a past event …

GRASS

This is the last time we were here.
Trampled on by sets of terrified feet.

FLEUR

I hear the panicked breaths of people.
I see where the feet tread and cross over.
Fire and smoke burn through the space,
slowing the moment to a terrified heart beat.
People scream and stare, eyes filled with fear.

GRASS

Our stems curl in upon ourselves,
huddling together in the refuge of the trees.
Frozen in fear, we do not think to move,
to hide our last few blades from angry fire.

FLEUR

A sharp light flashes, fire strikes.
I smell the scent of life burning.
I hear the torturous crying of loved ones,
clutching desperately at remnants of life.

GRASS

The north wind blows strongly.
Our few remaining gazes are transfixed
on the figure of our life-taker.
Standing tall against the fiery sky.

His last message is silent.
Not shared or spoken.
Marking our world with absence,
he chooses to walk away.

The north wind fumes.
We stretch our blades
with all our might,
reaching for our right to life.
And still we reach.

FLEUR

Staring up at the skies.
A streak of blood confronts me.

GRASS

You see that streak above us, Fleur?

FLEUR

Yes. Blood fire.

The smell of smoke remains,
a lingering warning.
I am shedding a tear for the loss
of our beloved world and people.

GRASS

Your skills are stronger than we realised.
You can see the blood.
It is the sign of things to come for us.

FLEUR

We must stop it.

GRASS

Listen beneath our blades, Fleur.
There is a message for you.

FLEUR

I am nature's new protector?

GRASS

Assist the tears of your loved ones, Fleur.
Renew and protect the land of your people.
Can we trust that you will help save us?

FLEUR

To be asked is an honour.
I will do all that I can.

Act 2, Scene 5

CELIA

Baby blue sky today with a small whisper of cloud.
My jean pocket is soaked.
That's right, I took a ham and salad sandwich
along for the ride out here.

You are still here in the aftermath, Veronique?
Here, in this meadow?
She is nodding, yes.
I don't think I will ever get her to speak to me.

The easel seems to have reappeared here, too.
It is propped up on one leg,
spinning in a dirt hole dug into the hill.
Wait a minute, is the hill flowering again?
Veronique is nodding, yes and pointing.
What is she pointing at?

The sun is very blinding.
I need to step into the shadows to see clearly.
Her figure is tall and surreal,
she has her arms raised up to the sky.
Beautiful Fleur, instinctively touching base
with her amazing nature skill.

Grass is flourishing across the hill and the meadow,
a sight I haven't seen for a long time.
Not since that terrifying day.

I guess it's time to repaint that picture
that I originally presented to Fleur and Sherwin.
I ended up erasing it off the canvas,
too painful a memory for the girl.

Where are the paints?
I see, they've been dug into the earth
in little ceramic pots, each with their own brush.
What colour do I begin with?

My brain, it doesn't seem to want to work these days.
What colour did they ask for?
Green, that's right, as green as the vibrant hill and meadow.
I'll begin with that.

AGAPANTHUS

We have brought the white dress with us, Veronique.
Celia managed to track it down in Fleur's aftermath.

It has a few burn holes in it.
Where do you want it?

VERONIQUE

On this counter, please.
I need to make some adjustments.

CELIA

Veronique is speaking to you?
How did that happen?

AGAPANTHUS

We are nature, a familiar part of her world.
She trusts us.

CELIA

She doesn't trust me?
Veronique, don't you trust me?
Are you shrugging?
What have I done wrong?

AGAPANTHUS

Nothing, Celia.
Veronique is protective of Fleur, she is her mother.
After all that's happened, she doesn't trust easily.

CELIA

I see.
Well, I'd better continue with this painting then, eh?
It might just help Fleur to remember …
Now, where is that pink paint?
The carnations, they were always so wild and free …

VERONIQUE

Can you try this dress on, Fleur?

FLEUR

That's the dress I keep seeing in my memories.
Why are there burn holes in it?

VERONIQUE

It was stuck in the smoky aftermath, Fleur.
There's nothing here that can't be patched up.

Let me just take your measurements.
Mmm. Some small adjustments are needed.
I'll do them now if you like.

FLEUR

I don't want to take the dress off, Maman.
It feels so comfortable on me, so right.
It was for something very special, wasn't it?

VERONIQUE

Oui, chère Fleur. Très spécial.   (Yes, dear Fleur. Very special.)

Something you and Sherwin have been planning for a long time.

FLEUR

Was it for a celebration, Maman?

VERONIQUE

Only of the best kind.

FLEUR

I want to walk in it for a while, Maman.
It might help me to remember.

VERONIQUE

Bien sûr, chère Fleur.   (Of course, dear Fleur).

FLEUR

The sun is continuing to rise, warming my soul.
I am treading across the Grass now,
enjoying its lush feeling beneath my feet.

GRASS

You look beautiful Fleur,
like an angel of nature.

FLEUR

Thank you Grass.
Will you keep me company?

GRASS

Of course.

FLEUR

I close my eyes and breathe in: 1,2,3 …
Exhaling: 4,5,6, I focus on the growth of the glass blades.
More blades begin to shoot, rolling their way across the plain.
I follow the new pathway, laughing as the grass tickles my bare feet.

CARNATION

You are amazing, Fleur.
There is hope yet.

FLEUR

Yes, hope.
What a lovely word.

A sudden image flashes in my mind of Girl.
She is wearing a lilac dress
and is bending down to pick some daisies.

Was this where we stood, enjoying those daisies?

GIRL

Yes, it was, Fleur.
Some time ago.
I think we might need some fresh flowers, don't you?

Step back, Fleur, I need to throw these stems into the air.

FLEUR

Wow! They are transforming!
I see daisies and carnations,
falling across the meadow and settling into the grass.

GIRL

The flowers will continue to bloom in the grass, Fleur.
Their heads and stems are connected once more.
They are back home now, where they belong.

FLEUR

So beautiful, so precious.
The petals are glistening in the sun.
Just like you.
Just like you always have.

I remember you now,
you're Petal, my best friend.

PETAL

Yes, I am.
Oh Fleur, I'm so happy that you remember me again.
Shall we pick some daisies for your celebration?

FLEUR

I wish I could remember what the celebration was for.

PETAL

Stand still Fleur.
Do not move.
It's happening again.

FLEUR

A flash of light blinds my eyes.
I see the outline of a figure, standing in the sun.
Is it Jarone?

PETAL

Yes, he's taken a photo of you, just like he did yesterday.

FLEUR

I took his original one, it's in my pocket.

PETAL

That's brave of you!
It's time to move!

FLEUR

We are running across the meadow, away from Jarone.
It is hard to move in this dress, I am tripping over its train.
Stopping for a moment, I place my hands on my knees,
bending to catch a breath.
I take the opportunity to observe Jarone.

He walks slowly and stops, staring at us.
I can see his eyes raging with fire.

PETAL

He wants something so bad,
he'll do anything to get it.

FLEUR

Yes, he does.
He won't get it though.
Not if I can help it.

PETAL
Where should we go?

FLEUR
Nowhere.
I'm not scared of you Jarone.
Can you see me stamping my feet?

You are frozen Jarone.
Your feet cannot budge out of the grass.

Your eyes still rage with fire.
Your lips form an evil smirk.

You lost something once, didn't you, Jarone?
Something very close and precious to you.
I know her, she is kind and beautiful,
her eyes can light up any room.

They still do actually, when she sees me.
She has not realised what state she exists in yet.
Roaming she is, searching for something far greater than wealth.
She desires peace.

CELIA
I have completed your painting, Fleur.
Come and see.

FLEUR
She speaks to me now, in my thoughts.
We have that connection, her and I.

CELIA
Who are you talking to, Fleur?

FLEUR
I am speaking to Jarone.

CELIA
My Jarone?

FLEUR
Yes.

CELIA

I am here, Fleur.
Stuck somewhere between the earth and sky,
trying to work out where I fit.

I see you Jarone.
You are only a fragment of the man I loved.
A snippet of yourself, trapped in a time travel,
lost somewhere between yesterday and now.

I feel your rage, Jarone.
It burns in your fiery eyes.
I am the girl you left behind,
after you chose to tear our world apart.

Leave Fleur and Sherwin alone.
This has nothing to do with them.
You need to travel back through time
and put the pieces of yourself together.

Somehow, after all you have done,
I still love you.
I want to help save you from yourself.
From what you are about to do again.

Come with me, Jarone.
This world does not need more damage.
It needs love.
An emotion you once felt for me.
Maybe somewhere, in a part of yourself, you still do.

FLEUR

Celia, are you sure you'll be okay?

CELIA

Yes Fleur.
Jarone is stuck, like me,
unsure how to rest.
He will never be able to
stay for long on this earth.
What you see of him now is only a projection.
It is a mere shade of his former self.

It is the angry, regretful shade
of a man who knew he went too far.

CELIA

Fleur, I leave you with this final gift,
a painting that you and Sherwin asked me to complete.
It is sitting, drying on the easel and is my gift to both of you
for your special celebration.
Best of luck to you, Fleur.

FLEUR

Goodbye my beautiful friend.
I hope to see you again.

CELIA

You can count on it.

Act 2, Scene 6

CELIA

Float with me, Jarone,
our travels are familiar together.
We stood upon this meadow once,
facing each other under the brightness of a full moon.

Your arms still feel so firm,
ready to reach out and pull me close to you.
Just like you did that night.

Can you feel me, Jarone?
It's your Celia, my body, pressing up against yours.

You have to be okay, just have to.
I know you are very afraid …
I am here for you.
I will help you breathe again, to recover …

If only I can stop being stuck
between the earth and the sky.
Maybe we could help each other
stamp out the fire that wrestles in our hearts.

JARONE

I see …

CELIA

Jarone? You are speaking?
What do you see?

JARONE

The flames rage in the darkness.
They are rising higher and higher …

Stop the screams!
Erase the faces that twist and distort,
as they fall and …

CELIA

You can't say the word, can you?
You're better than people think.
Jarone, I know you.
You are not responsible for this.

JARONE

Every day is too much,
it grinds and wears away at my soul.
To have the power to choose
what state I exist in,
what way I can be,
was once liberating ...
Now, all I can feel is such anger and pain.

ASH

Walk through us, Jarone.
We will show you a new way.
A life to begin from scratch,
without the burdens you carry
upon your heavy set shoulders.

You burn inside, Jarone.
She carries your deepest desire.
Yet she searches for another,
who she cannot quite reach.

CELIA

What makes you burn inside, Jarone?

ASH

She is not too far away,
walking towards the painting that Celia left behind.
She carries what you are after, Jarone.
A vial that buzzes with such life that it nearly
burns a whole in her pocket.

Go to her, Jarone.
Show her a new way.

CELIA

Fleur? You are after Fleur?
Stop now, Jarone.
Enough damage has been caused.

Look at me, your Celia.
The one you once pledged your love to
underneath the dazzling stars of night.

CELIA

I am still here for you, Jarone,
ready and willing to give you all that you need.
I am not afraid to love you.
Not anymore.
Let me soothe your anguish,
extinguish your fire …

Jarone!
Come back!

Act 2, Scene 7

FLEUR

What a beautiful painting.
Celia has captured the meadow of Sherwin and my hearts.
The hill is adorn with grass and flowers
and there we both are, hand in hand,
walking across it.

I am dressed in a white dress,
identical to what I am wearing.
You are walking behind us, Petal.

PETAL

Yes, I am carrying a beautiful bunch of daisies,
freshly picked from the meadow.
Daisies are so prolific, they need to be cut back from time to time.
You helped me to clear and to gather some of them, Fleur.
You even used some of the daisies to make my hair garland.

FLEUR

And so I did.
I have been remembering that moment.
We were both so happy, so excited.

PETAL

Yes, Fleur, we were.

FLEUR

Sherwin is wearing a suit, he looks so handsome.
It is strange though.

PETAL

What is, Fleur?

FLEUR

Well, he told me that he never got to see
me in my white dress as we planned.
We look happy in this picture.
I am wearing my white dress.

Did Sherwin lie to me?

PETAL

No, he didn't lie, Fleur.
The present is yet to unfold.
Not long now and you will see.
Can you see what is in the background of the painting?

FLEUR

Yes, the lake.
There is the glasshouse, right next to it.
It's sad that it is no longer here anymore.
Did someone knock it down?

PETAL

No, Fleur.

What you are about to witness will be difficult,
yet it will give you the answers you desire.

Do you wish to see what awaits?

FLEUR

Yes, if it will help to sort out this mess.
Will you come with me?

PETAL

I am afraid not, Fleur.
This is a journey you must take yourself.

Sherwin is waiting for you.
He is entering the glasshouse.

Go to him, Fleur.

FLEUR

Are you with me, Carnation?

CARNATION

I am, Fleur.
You can do this.

FLEUR

Yes, I can.

The grass feels delightful as its blades brush against my legs.
It is such a joy to venture through the wonders of the meadow.

CARNATION

Indeed it is, Fleur.
I am so happy to see new friends across the meadow and hill.

FLEUR

Can you see that, Carnation?

CARNATION

What is it, Fleur?

FLEUR

A building is taking shape before my eyes.
It is tall, with large windows.
It is the glasshouse.

There is Sherwin at the front door.

SHERWIN

Jarone!

FLEUR

Sherwin? What's going on?

SHERWIN

Fleur.
Wow.
You look beautiful.
I am not meant to see you before ...

Is it bad luck?

FLEUR

Maybe it is.

I remember now,
you did not arrive at the hill.
I was looking for you everywhere.
You met me here with such distress,
even though my heart soared with love.

My feet scuffed the ground,
beneath my beautiful, white dress.
I worried why you were so absent.

Did you have doubts, Sherwin?
It was meant to be our special day.

SHERWIN

I can't stand still, Fleur.
I must get inside.

FLEUR

Why do you want to leave me, Sherwin?
Why can't you just stay?

SHERWIN

Can you smell the smoke, Fleur?

FLEUR

Smoke?

Fire!

SHERWIN

Jarone! I'm coming to get you!
Aagh!

FLEUR

That door is heavy!

Here, let me help you up, Sherwin.
Whoa!

SHERWIN

The flames are strong, Fleur!
Stand back!

FLEUR

No, Sherwin.
I can face this.
It is something that I have already witnessed.
The smoke, the gold sparks …

I remember …
The radiant heater set alight.

SHERWIN

Looks like it.
Must be faulty wiring.

Jarone!

JARONE

Leave me be!
Save yourself!

SHERWIN

I can't do that, Jarone.

JARONE

I used you.
You have a right to be angry with me.

SHERWIN

That may be so.
Jarone! Watch out!

FLEUR

Celia?

The flames engulf the space, yet you stay.
Selfless, you are.

You reach for Jarone, yet he does not see.

CELIA

Jarone, please!
It's time to leave!

FLEUR

Let me get you out of here, Celia.

CELIA

I will not leave without my love, Jarone.
He is not a bad man, Fleur.
Just over ambitious, that's all.

Jarone, come with me, please!

JARONE

No! I will not leave my hybrid carnations behind.
Don't you see the future that can be had with these, Celia?
We will be wealthy and able to do all that we desire.

You, Fleur, give me that vial.

FLEUR

No, I will not!
Stop this craziness, Jarone!

SHERWIN

You leave her be!
You will never have that vial,
not while I can ever help it.

Snap out of it, Jarone.
Step outside now and save yourself.

JARONE

No!

CELIA

This fire propels Jarone,
it sparks him with determination.
He will not walk away easily.

If anyone can talk sense into him, it will be me.
Go now, both of you, before it is too late!

FLEUR

Celia, please!
Save yourself!

I can barely breathe.
The flames rage
and the smoke overpowers.

My legs feel wobbly.

SHERWIN

Fleur, Baby? Fleur?

FLEUR

Sherwin … ?

I am falling …
into the black.

Act 2, Scene 8

SHERWIN

Fleur?
Thank goodness, you're awake.

FLEUR

Sherwin?
You are holding me.
You are really here in the lake with me?

SHERWIN

Yes, I am.
This time we are both wading water and safe.

Yesterday was different Fleur,
I didn't walk away from the glasshouse.

That evening, I brought you down to the bank of this river.
However I left you out cold on the footbridge.
I thought you would be safe there.

Now I see that I was a mad man, running back,
leaving you here on your own.
I was trying to fight to save the others and the glasshouse.
I could not see reason.

By the time I got back here, you were gone.

After I floated through the air, searching for you,
I wound up wading in this water alone,
trying to soothe my terribly burnt skin.
Can you see my scars, Fleur?

FLEUR

Oh Sherwin, that must hurt.

What made you change your mind?

SHERWIN

The guilt has not left me Fleur.
For a long time I worried about you
and wanted to reach you.

Just before, in the glasshouse, you made me see sense.
I had to let it all go.

SHERWIN

Now I am mesmerised by the miracle of this present moment.
I have another chance to be with you, Fleur.
The glasshouse is gone and there is nothing I can do about it.
You are far more important to me.

FLEUR

And you to me, Sherwin.

SHERWIN

I love you, Fleur.

FLEUR

I love you too.

SHERWIN

I know this was meant to be our special day, Fleur.
Under this wondrous sky, amid the romantic, falling leaves,
I feel brave enough to ask you once more.

FLEUR

Sherwin?

SHERWIN

Will you let me have the honour of being my wife?

FLEUR

Yes, yes, yes!

SHERWIN

Oh, Fleur. You have made me the happiest man in the universe.

FLEUR

For the first time in a long while, I am truly happy, Sherwin.
To think that we can continue to tread together,
across the landscape of our lives.
There is nothing more that I could ever ask for.

SHERWIN

Oh Fleur. I am so lucky to have you in my life.
I will never take it for granted again.

FLEUR

Promise?

SHERWIN
Solemnly.

FLEUR
I have an idea, Sherwin.

SHERWIN
What is it?

FLEUR
I know that we can't change what happened
but maybe we can help the meadow and lake to have stronger futures.
Could we share some of the pollen in this vial with nature?

SHERWIN
What a great idea, Fleur.
The pollen was originally from this meadow.

Nature has suffered enough.
I'm sure it will appreciate the help.

FLEUR
Closing my eyes, I make a wish and release the pollen into the air.
Watching it float, I am relieved.
The burnt trees of the lake are slowly recovering,
their leaves unfurling and becoming green again.

New, wild carnations are budding across the grass.

CARNATION
Wow! The wild carnations have returned!
You are amazing, Fleur!

SHERWIN
Your heart's desire is truly beautiful, Fleur.

FLEUR
Yes.
Should we help the hill, Carnation?

CARNATION
Oh yes, that would be wonderful.

FLEUR

Walk with me, both of you.
My hand feels so safe in yours, Sherwin.
I see now, the picture Celia painted,
is of this special moment in the present,
where you chose to stay with me, Sherwin.

There is Petal, following closely behind us.

PETAL

You did it, Fleur.
Well done!

FLEUR

Yes, we all did.

I offer this hill and our meadow, some pollen,
to help it continue to flourish and grow.

In the wild we discover our instincts and our truths.
In this moment, I make a solemn promise to
live in harmony with the wild
and to never interfere with its natural course.
It is much braver and sturdier than we realise
and can withstand almost anything.

SHERWIN

Just like us, Fleur.

CARNATION

Just like me.

FLEUR

Yes, just like all of us.

Some moments are worth holding onto forever.
I see the joyous sun glinting in my love's eyes and in Petal's hair.
I see the way that Carnation smiles radiantly at me.

We are all here, alive and well, together.

I feel euphoric happiness as we continue to walk
across the meadow of our present and future.

The world will be as is and I can't wait for our continued journey together.

The End.

About the Author

 **Susan Marshall** is a novelist, fiction writer, poet and dramatist and the founder of Story Playscapes. She is also a theatre practitioner and an expert educator. Susan is highly skilled in working with young adults in theatrical, educational and community settings and is a recipient of a prestigious award for her outstanding and extensive work with young people.

Susan's love for the arts began in early childhood. She discovered she had a strong physical connection with her surroundings (her playscapes) and could work with moments of energetic motions, letting them breathe and take flight through writing and performance work. She has fond memories of her parents encouraging her to read and write stories. She would also decorate her backyard with sheets as curtains and invite her parents as audience members to share in her performance work.

Susan's first productions were in primary school, under the experienced guidance of her significant teachers: Kim Young and Stu Cooper. She portrayed the Narrator in the stage adaptation of Road Dahl's *James and the Giant Peach*. In her French studies, she also had the fortune to portray the King in the French stage adaptation of *Le Petit Prince* by Antoine de Saint-Exupéry.

In secondary school, Susan felt blessed to be taught English and Drama by Di Gagen, the professional Australian theatre critic and stage director. Di was instrumental in helping Susan to discover and harness her artistic nature and skills. Under Di's guidance, Susan learnt how to critique live theatrical performance and to further develop and refine her writing skills.

Di Gagen also trained Susan in the art of theatre direction, by allowing her to take on the role of Stage Director for the productions: *Just Equal* by Dennis Betts and *A Midsummer Night's Dream* by William Shakespeare. Susan also had the privilege of being taught the skills of professional pantomimic performance when she was cast as various roles, including Phoebe and a Field Mouse in A. A. Milne's *Toad of Toad Hall*, which was co-directed by Di and Steve Gagen at the Hartwell Players in Melbourne.

Di Gagen also introduced Susan to the world of St Martin's Youth Arts Centre in Melbourne. Susan spent many years there, further developing her skills in performance. She was privileged to be trained in the techniques of improvisation by the experienced Geoff Wallis and even participated in a number of *Theatresports* regional finals.

Another highlight for Susan at St Martin's Youth Arts Centre, was the opportunity to be trained by the professional actor, James Wardlaw, in Stanislavski's method acting techniques. Susan also worked closely with the highly esteemed Artistic Director, Brett Adam, on devising and writing the script for the production of *Orb.IT* for the Melbourne International Arts Festival. As an actor, Susan also enjoyed portraying various roles in the non-realistic production within the modern set design created by Darryl Cordell.

Susan attended La Trobe University, where she completed a Bachelor of Arts and majored in English and Theatre and Drama. In her English degree, she committed herself to learning to read, analyse and write a range of narrative types, from classical to post structuralist. Professor Richard Freadman was a significant lecturer for Susan, due to his encouragement of her reading and analysis skills in autobiographical texts; along with broadening her understandings of the notions of the self in writing and literary theory.

In her Theatre and Drama degree, Susan was fortunate to be taught the art of theatre performance and theory by the highly experienced and esteemed, late Geoffrey Milne. She was also blessed to learn from the amazing expertise of the theatre practitioners: Julian Meyrick, Peta Tait and Meredith Rogers.

At La Trobe University, Susan also enjoyed portraying various roles in the theatrical production: *As You Like It*, by William Shakespeare, directed by Meredith Rogers and performed at the Trades Hall in Melbourne. She also performed the protagonist in the post structuralist production of Virginia Baxter's *What Time is This House?* at the Melbourne Fringe Festival. Later, she performed Phrygenia in the production *Spartacus and Phrygenia*, (written and directed by Peter and Corinne at Créations Barquette Gitane), for the Banyule Festival in Melbourne.

Keen to learn more about theatre direction, Susan had the privilege of observing and being taught by the professional stage director, Richard Keown, as he directed the Australian premiere production of John Harrison's *Holidays* at Peridot Theatre in Melbourne. Later, Susan had the privilege of directing the Australian premiere production of Timothy Daly's *Beach: A Theatrical Fantasia* with a young cast.

Always passionate about the arts and wanting to share her knowledge with young people, Susan completed a postgraduate Bachelor of Education: Primary and Secondary, at Deakin University and was privileged to learn from the expertise of her amazing lecturers: Dr Jo O'Mara and Dr Jo Raphael.

Susan has taught professionally in primary and secondary schools for more than a decade and has undertaken the role of Head of Drama. Susan has also written a number of drama and literacy articles for academic publications and mentored pre-service and practising teachers. She has presented at state and national conferences in drama and literacy education, including at the Victorian College of the Arts, the University of Melbourne and at the Queensland University of Technology in Brisbane and has also worked as an executive committee member for Drama Victoria.

As time progressed, Susan immersed herself in the adventures of play writing with the intention of developing works for young adults to explore in the classroom or youth theatre settings. This led to the development of her play: *Broken World*, which was published by RMDesigned in 2013. The play was launched at the joint AATE/ALEA National Conference and positively reviewed by the Children's Book Council of Australia. RMDesigned also published Susan's second play, *Indigo's Haven* in 2016.

Susan has also written a range of publications, which have been published at Vocal Media in the U.S.A. These include, Susan's poems: *Grandpa Ben's Mysterious Notebook: A Tale; A Day Spent: the Playful Thoughts of a Tired Mind; My Nature Spirit: A Poem Celebrating my Connection with Nature; Is Summer Still Aglow Within Thy Heart?: The Eternal Shore of Summer Love; Winter's Breath: Mother Nature's Precious Time* and *Heart's Land*, along with her short stories: *Paper Jilu: A Journey of Her Notes; Gail's Red Horizon: A Fantastical Adventure; Hidden Magic: Part 1; Peonies for Masha: Her Journey Home* (shortlisted as a finalist in the Vocal+ Fiction Awards, 2022); *Stay* and *Tace's Lost Spirit: Searching for Vie.*

Susan is an honoured recipient of the prestigious *Award for Special Civic Service*, which was presented to her by the Mayor of Richmond, Victoria, for her extensive civic contributions to the city of Richmond and the Richmond City Council. The Award particularly recognises her outstanding efforts in assisting young people through her work on the Richmond Youth Work Project and the Richmond Youth Council.

In 2020, Susan founded Story Playscapes, her writing and publishing business. It was here that she became globally renown for delving into her playscapes when developing her writing. Susan's written works are highly respected by a dedicated global audience.

As an author, theatre practitioner and educator, Susan brings a wealth of knowledge to Story Playscapes. She is passionate about empowering literacy development in her global readership. Susan is also big hearted in her discussions on social media, where she fosters a love for reading and discovery in her readers.

In 2022, Susan was privileged to collaborate with the world class designer, Ryan Marshall, on the book design of her debut novel: *Makeshift Girl: The Secret Heritage Trail*. A literary fiction, it is book one of the Makeshift Girl series and is also Susan's debut novel for adults. The Hardcover Collector's Edition also includes the publication of her Romantic poem: *Evergold Dream*. The novel was released on February 17, 2023, to book retailers and readers around the globe.

In 2023, Susan has continued her collaboration with Ryan Marshall and is honoured that he has designed her new play publication for young adults: *Fleur of Yesterday*. It is the first play in Story Playscapes' new Theatre Playscapes series. In the publication, Susan is also proud to officially present her monumental achievement: her new Theatre Playscapes theatrical style, developed for young performers, to readers and theatre makers around the world.

Acknowledgements

In creating this book, I acknowledge the wonderful presence and growth of young people in our world. In presenting the new Theatre Playscapes theatrical style and *Fleur of Yesterday*, I aim to provide our young people with opportunities to nurture their own senses of beings and lifeworlds in theatre.

I wish to thank the people of the Luberon villages in France, for inviting me to share in moments of their lifeworlds. I have learnt so much and grown spiritually as a result of my time spent travelling and engaging with you.

I wish to thank the global readership of Story Playscapes. Your support and encouragement has been highly appreciated as I worked on this book.

A special thank you to Ryan Marshall, my amazing collaborator, who has drawn upon his world class expertise to produce the stunning photography, digital art and design work for this book.

About the Book Designer

Ryan Marshall is a graphic designer, photographer and illustrator, with more than 20 years of experience in designing a broad range of monographs, trade and fiction publications for world-leading professionals in the arts, design, photographic, automotive, landscape design and architectural industries.

Ryan has applied his unique technical skill set to the design and creation of hundreds of titles and includes significant contributions to international bestselling publications and series.

In 2022, Ryan collaborated with Susan Marshall and designed Story Playscapes' premiere publication: *Makeshift Girl: The Secret Heritage Trail.* The novel was released in February, 2023 and is currently available at book retailers around the globe. Ryan is delighted to bring his highly proficient design and technical expertise to the book design, photography and digital art for *Fleur of Yesterday* by Susan Marshall.

It is a rewarding experience for Ryan to collaborate with Susan and to bring her wonderful stories to the printed page for readers to discover and enjoy!

About Story Playscapes

Story Playscapes, established in 2020, is an Australian writing and publishing business founded by Australian Author, Susan Marshall.

The business is dedicated to promoting positive approaches to literacy development. It nurtures a global readership by actively sharing Susan Marshall's diverse range of written works on its website and via print and ebook publications.

Susan also communicates regularly with her readers via social media, encouraging them to develop a love for reading and discovering the story.

In 2023, Story Playscapes released its premiere publication: *Makeshift Girl: The Secret Heritage Trail* by Susan Marshall. It is book one of the Makeshift Girl series and is also Susan's debut novel for adults. The Hardcover Collector's Edition also includes the publication of her Romantic poem: *Evergold Dream.* The novel is currently available at retailers around the globe.

In this beautiful paperback edition, *Story Playscapes* is proud to celebrate Susan Marshall's monumental achievement: her Theatre Playscapes theatrical style and her new play, *Fleur of Yesterday.* It is the exciting first play in the new Theatre Playscapes series.

Story Playscapes

DISCOVER THE STORY

🌐 www.storyplayscapes.com

ⓕ Facebook: /storyplayscapes

⊙ Instagram: @storyplayscapes